trouble on mars

travis & trouble
book two

Henry Vogel

Published in the United States of America by Moranderin Media, an imprint of VL Publishing.

Cover art by Miblart.com.

First publication: June 2023

ISBN: 978-1-959859-14-7 (ebook)

ISBN: 978-1-959859-15-4 (hardback)

ISBN: 978-1-959859-23-9 (paperback)

Originally published in serial form online.

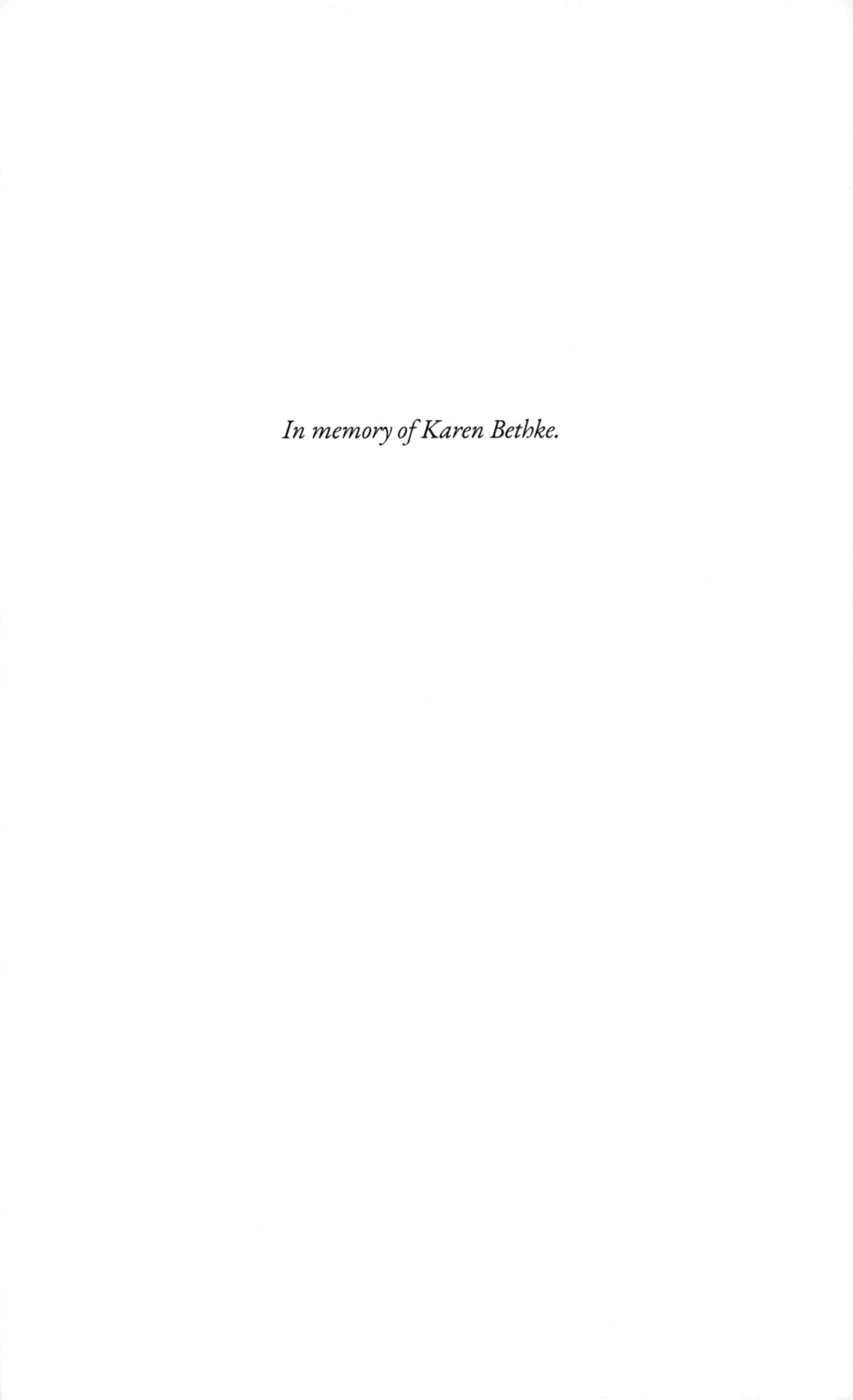

In memory of Karen Bethke.

trouble with intelligence

I **STOOD** for a moment and watched Trouble stride purposefully past the men working on our soon-to-be shared office. As she disappeared into the morning foot traffic beyond our door, I grabbed our two suitcases and followed her. But a man stepped into the office door and blocked my way. He was about my size and spacer pale, which made his dark hair and eyes appear even darker.

In a tone so smooth it made me want to check my wallet, the man asked, "Going somewhere, Barrett?"

"Out," I said, and twisted to shoulder past him.

"Why would you want to do that?" He put his left hand on my chest and pushed.

I spent the last two weeks worried about ex-heavyweight boxer Hammerhand Houlihan. This new guy wasn't even close to Hammerhand's weight class. I stiff armed him with a suitcase. He stumbled back, and I swung the other suitcase around and knocked his left arm away. I spun around the man, gave him a two suitcase shove to the side, and kept moving towards the doorway.

And found my way blocked again, this time by an attractive young woman in a stylish business suit. I slowed, unwilling to plow through her the same way I did her friend.

"There's no reason to make this difficult, Mr. Barrett." She smiled. "We just want to talk with you."

"Call my office and make an appointment," I said, and turned sideways to edge around her. "I don't have time right now."

"You don't have time for an old academy buddy?" the man asked.

I turned, gave the man a closer look, and thought he looked familiar. I searched my memory for a name to go with the face, and finally came up with one. "McGill?"

He nodded. "In the flesh."

I gave the woman a closer look, noticed her red hair for the first time, but I didn't recognize her. She confirmed that when she said, "We've never met, Mr. Barrett. You graduated from the Space Patrol Academy before I enrolled."

They weren't in uniform, so I asked, "Are you on active duty?"

"Yeah," McGill said.

"No uniforms, so... Space Patrol Intelligence Force?" At their nods, I asked, "What do a pair of Spiffies want with me?"

McGill glanced at the workmen, all of whom had stopped working and were watching us with interest. He nodded his head towards the back office. "How about a little privacy before we get into that?"

I nodded at the crowd outside. "People are waiting for me."

"This won't take long," the woman said.

I put down a suitcase and pulled out my comm. "Then you won't mind if I comm them first."

McGill shrugged, and the woman said, "Not at all." I raised an eyebrow in surprise, which prompted her to add, "We're not your enemy, Mr. Barrett."

"You're not my friends, either," I said, and tapped in Trouble's comm code.

Trouble answered with a bright, "Hi, Travis."

"I'm going to be a little late getting to the ship," I said. "An old academy acquaintance showed up as I was leaving."

Her voice sharpened. "Is it Jacobson?"

"No," I said, "he wouldn't have let me comm you. He's also on Space Patrol's Most Wanted list, and isn't stupid enough to show his face on Carnegie Station."

"You're saying there's no danger from your visitors?"

"I don't think so."

"Then I'm coming back there."

I thought that was the exact opposite of what McGill and his partner wanted, so said, "Sure. We'll be in the back office. Just walk on in when you get here."

The woman frowned. "We only want to talk to you, Barrett."

I headed for the back office. "Tough."

They followed me into the office. McGill shut the door, and said, "We're here on official Space Patrol business. It's not for civilian ears."

"Darn, I guess that means you can't tell me, either," I said.

McGill rolled his eyes. "You're Space Patrol, Barrett."

"Not anymore, I'm not."

"Surely you have a sense of service loyalty?" the woman asked.

"To Space Patrol?"

She nodded.

"The same Space Patrol that court-martialled me for the heinous crime of doing my duty?" I asked.

"Now, Mr. Barrett—"

"And did *not* court martial Jacobson, the cowardly commander who let my ship and crew take on the solar system's worst pirate ship alone? You mean *that* Space Patrol?"

"Neither of us had anything to do with that." The woman added, "And this outburst isn't helping, Mr. Barrett."

"It's no longer my job to help Space Patrol."

She crossed her arms. "You don't mean that."

"With all my heart."

"Look, Barrett," McGill growled, "this is important."

"Cut to the chase and tell me what you want," I said. "Then I can refuse and be on my way."

McGill balled his fists. "Just shut up for a minute and let us explain."

"I'm not interested in explanations." I reached for the suitcases. "Give me the bottom line or I walk."

"Okay," the woman said. "Take me with you to Mars."

I stared at the woman and tried to make sense of her request. "Look, Miss...?"

"Captain Marian Stark," she replied.

I raised one eyebrow. "You're going to blow your Spiffy cover, if that's how you introduce yourself."

"That is how I introduce myself to allies, Mr. Barrett. You should call me Miss Stark when anyone else is present."

"Whether I call you Captain Stark or Miss Stark doesn't matter. What matters is that you're a member of Space Patrol, owners of the largest space fleet in the solar system. Why can't the Spiffy brass send you to Mars on a Space Patrol ship?"

McGill growled, "We're trying to keep this on the down low, Barrett. That's hard to do if Captain Stark arrives on one of our boats."

"I thought you had all sorts of Spiffy spy stuff to get around problems like that," I said.

"Stop working 'Spiffy' into every sentence, Barrett," McGill said. "It's not clever, and it gets old real fast."

"Is that an order, Spiffy Super Spy McGill, sir?" I asked.

McGill reddened, and drew breath for a retort, but Stark said, "May we please return to the topic at hand, gentlemen?"

I saw the door open behind the two Space Patrollers. Trouble slipped into the office and softly closed the door again. For her benefit, I said, "That's a good idea. Why don't you restate your request, Captain Stark, and we'll go from there?"

She nodded and said, "Space Patrol wants you to take me to Mars."

"Why?" I asked.

"Isn't it obvious, Travis?" Trouble asked.

McGill and Stark whirled around and stared at Trouble. Then McGill asked, "When did you get here?"

Trouble leaned against the door and folded her arms. "Just before Travis asked your associate to restate her request."

"And what is so obvious about my request?" Stark asked.

Trouble patted her hair and smiled.

"Yeah, I noticed her red hair," I said.

"Have you figured out Space Patrol wants her to pretend she's a Traveller?" Trouble asked.

"I was getting there," I said. I looked at Stark. "How long has Spiffy been training you in Martian culture?"

"Spiffy?" Trouble asked.

"Space Patrol Intelligence Force," Stark said. "My training is far from complete, but the opportunity you and Mr. Barrett have is too good for my superiors to pass up."

"So, I figure you want more from us than just a ride to Mars?" I asked.

Stark nodded. "Our covert operations team is putting together a cover for me as we speak. They're making stuff up on the fly, so it won't stand up to close scrutiny. But the Martian representatives in Marsport don't have the resources an Earth government has, so it should stand up well enough."

I shook my head. "We're not dealing with the Martian government."

"There isn't a single Martian government, Barrett," McGill said. "But all the big local governments send representatives to the Martian Council. It's like the Martian version of our United Planets."

"Call it whatever you like," I said. "It changes nothing. We're dealing with a bar owner named Mah'Ri."

McGill smirked. "Otherwise known as the Martian Council representative from Kah'Freon."

Trouble and I exchanged startled glances, then both asked, "What?"

"She's been a fixture in Marsport for decades, Mr. Barrett,"

Stark said. "Outside of Marsport, everything on Mars is closed to Earthers. The representatives have little to do beyond collect taxes and deny requests to visit the rest of the planet. We assume running the bar is Mah'Ri's way of filling her free time."

"Okay..." I said. "So, um, you want to pretend you're a Traveller, and hope Mah'Ri will let you tag along with us on whatever it is she wants me to investigate?"

"Exactly," Stark said.

"She might want me for a local case."

"We don't think so," McGill said.

"Would you care to elaborate?" I asked.

"No."

"Then we're done here." I looked at Trouble. "Ready to go?"

"Please wait. Our source is a deep-cover agent." She met my gaze with hard, cold eyes. "If the wrong word is spoken in the wrong place, our agent's life is forfeit and his intel will be rendered useless."

McGill's face paled. "Christ."

"Didn't you already know that?" I asked.

Instead of answering, McGill glanced at Stark. She nodded, and he said, "I don't work with Captain Stark. My commanding officer ordered me to come with her because I knew you at the Academy. I tried telling them we barely knew each other, but you know how the brass can be when they latch onto an idea."

"Typical Spiffy operation," I snorted. "Damned if I know why you call it an intelligence service, because it sounds like that's one thing sorely lacking over there."

McGill shrugged. "Look, Barrett, I—"

With authority previously missing from her voice, Stark said, "You're dismissed, Lieutenant Commander."

"Yes, ma'am," McGill said. "Shall I wait outside?"

"No," Stark said. "Return to your normal duties."

Without another word, McGill left the room. Stark waited half-a-minute after the door closed, then she said, "Please give me your oath that what I'm about to tell you will stay between the three of us."

Trouble turned an inquiring look my way. I nodded, and said, "You have my word."

"And mine," Trouble said.

"Thank you," Stark said. "Our deep cover agent has worked his way onto the support crew for the *Bloodsword*. He reports that the ship's base is on Mars."

Images of my one-sided battle with that terrifying pirate ship filled my mind. The dying screams of my crew echoed in my ears. I glared at Stark. "You'd have saved a lot of time if you led with that. Do you think you can bring the *Bloodsword's* crew to justice?"

"I wouldn't be here if I didn't," she said.

I gave a decisive nod. "I'm in."

"Since Travis is in, I'm in, too," Trouble said.

Captain Stark acknowledged our statements with a nod. "Excellent. I'll have the pilot bring my things to the *Lightning's Hand*."

My eyebrows rose in surprise. "What pilot?"

"A SPIF-trained pilot, of course." Stark offered what I assume was supposed to be a confident smile. "Don't worry, he's the best one in SPIF."

"We already have a pilot." I flashed a confident smile of my own. "Don't worry, he's better than anyone Space Patrol has to offer."

Stark's smile faded. "Mr. Hayslett's talents are not in question. But he is unsuitable for this job."

"Elaborate," Trouble said.

"SPIF has its reasons," Stark replied. "You'll just have to trust—"

"I wasn't making a request," Trouble said.

Stark looked at me. "Mr. Barrett, please control your employee, or—"

I picked up our suitcases and started for the office door. "That's it, Stark. We're out."

"You cannot be serious?" Stark said.

"As serious as a blaster cannon shot up the engine tubes, Captain." I put down one suitcase and reached for the doorknob. "Goodbye."

In a cold, hard tone, Stark said, "I cannot believe you, of all people, can turn your back on the opportunity to avenge the crew members who died under your command. Unlike Hayslett, you're no coward. You—"

I dropped the other suitcase and whirled to face Stark. My expression must have conveyed my feelings, because Stark's face paled. I stalked towards her, and she backpedaled from me, stopping only when she hit the far wall.

I advanced until our chests touched and glared down into her gray eyes. "Have you ever been in combat, Stark?"

Stark straightened and used her command voice. "Step back, Mr. Barrett."

Her tone might have worked on someone else, but I had my own command voice. "Answer the question, Patroller."

We held each other's gaze for another ten seconds, then Stark's glare faded and she looked down. "No."

"Then I strongly suggest you refrain from passing your ignorant judgement on Patrollers who have proved themselves repeatedly in the line of duty."

Stark didn't look into my eyes again, but she didn't retreat from our confrontation. "I am merely repeating Hayslett's own assessment of himself. Perhaps you were unaware—"

"Dave told me everything when we were on Mercury. How *you* know of it, is a different question."

"I'm with SPIF, Mr. Barrett. It's our job to know these things. Since you also know of Hayslett's confession, you must understand Space Patrol's opinion of him."

"No, I mustn't. Do you want to know why?"

Stark tried a nonchalant wave of her hand, but I was too close for her to pull it off. "Fine. Tell me."

"Because the *only* reason I'm here right now is because of Dave Hayslett."

"You said as much multiple times during your court martial, Mr. Barrett."

"I'm not talking about the *Soteria's* battle with the *Bloodsword*."

Stark vented an exasperated sigh. "Then what are you talking about?"

"Mercury."

"What about Mercury?"

"While Space Patrol cooperated with the criminals holding me hostage, Dave staged a one-man rescue. Then he helped me rescue my friends and associates from Space Patrol. The same Space Patrol whose opinion of Dave you think I should accept without question."

"Come now, Barrett," Stark said, "you can't seriously judge the whole of Space Patrol based on the actions of a few corrupt Patrollers."

"Why not? You're judging Dave based on words spoken six years ago, while ignoring actions from less than a week ago."

Stark raised her eyes and stared into mine for a moment. "You may be right, but I have my orders. And I can't believe you will pass up the opportunity to finally put an end to the *Bloodsword* and her crew."

"You're right, I won't pass it up." I backed away from Stark. "I'll just find the pirates on my own."

Stark looked past me. "Miss Tate, please talk some sense into Mr. Barrett?"

I turned around and watched a devilish smile form on Trouble's lips. "Why? You're the one who keeps spouting nonsense."

In an incredulous tone, Stark asked, "You're going along with this foolish idea?"

"It doesn't sound foolish to me," Trouble said.

"You're both daft! Mars is a *planet*. You could spend the rest of your lives searching it, and still never find the pirates' base."

"You came to us for a reason, and it's not because some Martians think Miss Tate is a Traveller." I shook my head. "No, I think you came to us because Mah'Ri wants me to investigate something for her. That means we can concentrate our search on Mah'Ri's home of Kah'Freon."

"If you do that, you'll ruin our operation," Stark said, "get our agent killed, and probably yourselves, as well. Are you willing to do that over one pilot?"

"I suggest you ask yourself the same question," Trouble said.

Stark was silent for half-a-minute. "Give me until tomorrow. I'll have to get this approved by my superiors."

"You have two hours." I picked up our suitcases. "If you aren't onboard the *Lightning's Hand* by then, we're leaving without you." As Trouble opened the office door for me, I looked back at Stark. "Oh, bring proper ID and orders, or we won't let you onboard."

Ninety minutes later, Captain Marian Stark presented her documentation to me, and boarded the *Lightning's Hand*. Then we set sail for Mars.

two
trouble with cover stories

CAPTAIN STARK SPENT the first hour settling into her cabin. Trouble took care of what little settling our cabin required, while Rita and I examined Stark's orders in minute detail. Rita has a database of Space Patrol law and legal precedents, something I had her download when she began working for me, and I had her look up everything in the orders that was open to interpretation.

Trouble joined me as I worked my way through the last page of Stark's three-page written orders. When I pushed the pages aside and sat back, she asked, "Do Captain Stark's orders match the story she gave us?"

"As best I can tell, yes." I sighed. "The orders are long on generalities and short on specifics. Meaning she has a hell of a lot of latitude."

Stark entered the room. "What did you expect, Mr. Barrett? Undercover work involves fluid situations that require a level of flexibility not found in traditional operations." She cocked her head as if in thought, then said, "My work is much like the search and rescue work you and your crew performed on the *Soteria*. I expect your orders included the last known position of the ship, its design, the crew roster, and the passenger list. But the orders didn't include how to perform the search, nor how to rescue people from the ship when you found it."

"That's true," I said, "but your orders amount to little more than 'find the *Bloodsword's* base and neutralize the pirates.' That's a lot of responsibility for a lone captain on her first independent assignment."

"But I'm not alone, Mr. Barrett. I have you and Miss Tate assisting me."

"And Dave," Trouble added.

"Mr. Hayslett is the pilot," Stark replied. "I won't depend on him for anything else."

"Is that so?" I asked.

"It is, Mr. Barrett. I have specific orders to that effect."

"No, you don't." I tapped the written orders with my index finger. "I read every line in these orders, and nothing in there refers to Dave by name or allusion."

"It was a spoken order," Stark replied.

"And you were planning on telling us about that order when?" I asked.

"I just told you."

"Only because I questioned your claim. What other spoken orders did you receive?"

"None."

"Why should I believe you?" I waved my question off before Stark answered, and asked, "How are you going to stop Dave from taking part in this mission?"

"I hoped you would convince him to remain with the ship."

I glared at Stark and waited for her to backpedal from that idea. She met my glare with an impassive expression and remained silent. After half-a-minute, I raised my voice and called, "Hey, Dave?"

"Yeah?" he yelled.

"Do you want to stay with the *Lightning's Hand* while Trouble, Stark, and I go after the pirates?"

"Hell no!"

"Are you sure?"

"Damn straight."

I smiled at Stark, shrugged, and said, "I tried, but I can't convince him."

Stark's glare intensified. "I believe you have seriously underestimated the dangers involved in this operation, Mr. Barrett."

"I doubt it. But you have seriously underestimated what a man will do to absolve himself of past sins."

Stark leaned back in her chair. "You had better be right about Mr. Hayslett."

I sat back, crossed my arms, and said, "I am."

Stark nodded her head at Trouble. "Enough to risk her life, along with the mission?"

"I can speak for myself, and I agree with Travis," Trouble said. "Now, let's put this discussion behind us and move on to something more productive. For starters, perhaps you could share your plan for convincing Mah'Ri to let you accompany us beyond Marsport's boundary?"

"What's to say?" Stark replied. "You already know the plan. All we have to do is tell Mah'Ri I'm like you, another Traveller returning to Mars. It doesn't get much simpler than that."

"Well," I said, "it's obvious this is another Spiffy plan concocted on the spur of the moment."

"What do you expect?" Stark asked. "We only learned of your promise to return to Mars and perform a job for Mah'Ri yesterday. Even this minimal plan was only possible because I was already in training for insertion as a Traveller."

"Your plan won't work," I said.

"It will if you and Miss Tate help me sell it."

I shook my head. "Wrong."

"Please explain?" Stark asked.

"I already tried using the Traveller story on Mah'Ri," Trouble said. "She told us she follows the ancient religion of Mars, and doesn't believe Travellers are Martian souls reincarnated in Earther bodies."

Stark remained silent for several seconds, then suggested, "Then you must say whatever it takes to convince Mah'Ri to let me go with you. Maybe tell her you hired me as another assistant.?"

"Mah'Ri trusts me to tell her the truth," I said. "I won't betray that trust."

"Then just stay silent and let me tell the lies," Stark said.

"Mah'Ri isn't stupid, Stark," I snapped. "The first thing she'll do is ask me if your story is true. And I will not lie to her."

"Then there's no point in me even coming with you," Stark said.

"I think you're underestimating Mah'Ri," Trouble said.

Stark turned her glare on Trouble. "Oh really? And what's *your* brilliant plan to convince Mah'Ri to let me go with you?"

"I know this is probably heresy for an intelligence operative," Trouble said, "but why don't you simply tell Mah'Ri the truth?"

Stark stared at Trouble in astonishment. "You want me to tell Mah'Ri the truth?"

"Yes," Trouble said.

"That I'm a covert operative from the Space Patrol Intelligence Force, hoping she'll help me skirt all the Martians' security procedures, giving me free rein to roam her restricted planet?"

Trouble folded her arms. "Again, yes."

Stark vented an exasperated sigh. "What part of *covert* do you not understand, Miss Tate?"

"We explained why your original plan won't work, Captain Stark," Trouble countered. "What part of that do *you* not understand?"

Stark opened her mouth to reply, then closed it again as her face assumed an unexpected expression. A thoughtful one. After a moment, she turned to me. "Are you certain there's no other way to gain Mah'Ri's trust?"

I sought a gentle tone and said, "Lies do not engender trust, Marian."

Her lips quirked up in a half-smile. "That's the first time you've used my given name."

"I thought it would get your attention, without also putting you on the defensive."

Marian nodded her understanding. "I'll need to discuss this with my superiors."

I waved towards the cockpit. "The comm is all yours."

"Thank you, but I have an encrypted comm in my luggage." She headed for her cabin. "This isn't a discussion for an open channel."

After Marian's door slid shut, Trouble asked, "Do you think her boss will allow it?"

"Maybe." I headed for the ship's bar and poured a scotch for Trouble and me. "It's not like we're giving them much choice."

We settled on the sofa. Trouble kissed me gently and asked, "How are you doing, Travis?"

"Don't worry about me."

Rita spoke for the first time since Marian came from her cabin. "You're avoiding the question again, Boss."

"Nobody asked you, Rita," I growled.

A smug expression lit Rita's face screen. "That never stopped me before."

I pretended to consider an idea. "You know, I bet Trouble is rich enough that we can afford a new, top-of-the-line Robosec. One with all the best secretarial modules and a respectful attitude."

"You know I'd never do that, Travis," Trouble said. "Rita's family."

Rita's expression flowed from smug to delighted, and her face screen brightened. "Thanks, Miss Boss, ma'am!"

"You're welcome, Rita." Trouble turned her attention back to me. "You didn't answer my question, Travis."

I knocked back my scotch. "Sure, I did."

Trouble caught my chin and turned my head until we faced

each other. Warm blue eyes caught my gaze. "Please answer my question."

"I'm not sure. I never thought I'd ever get a chance to bring the *Bloodsword* and her crew to justice, but suddenly, here it is." I leaned my head back and sighed. "What if I blow it? What if the pirates get away, set up a new base somewhere else in the solar system, and continue terrorizing the space lanes?"

"Then things will be exactly as they are now. But..." Trouble rested her head on my shoulder. "What if you *don't* blow it? What if the pirates are captured and their ship destroyed? Have you considered that?"

"Only every day since the *Bloodsword* destroyed the *Soteria*. But I—"

"Why do you keep saying *I*?" Trouble interrupted. "You aren't in this alone, Travis, so stop trying to shoulder all the responsibility. And maybe you should start saying *we* more often?"

"I'll try, but I've been alone for so long it might take years to change."

"Hey," Rita squawked, "you ain't been alone since you bought me, Boss."

"Rita has a good point," Trouble said. "But now you have Dave and me, too."

The ship's intercom crackled, and Dave said, "What she said, Travis. Only, you better not expect me to sleep with you."

"I'd pay good money to avoid that, Dave," I replied.

"Yeah?" he asked. "How much?"

Trouble laughed. "I won't share my man, Dave."

"So," Dave mused, "how much will *you* pay me not to sleep with Travis?"

Before Trouble came up with an answer, Marian's cabin door slid open and she rejoined us. Trouble cocked an eyebrow and asked, "What did your superior say?"

Marian dropped into a chair. "He expressly forbade me to reveal my identity to Mah'Ri, or to tell her about my mission."

"I suppose that is a typical Spiffy spy move," I said. "Are they sending a Patrol cruiser to rendezvous with us, so you can go back to training?"

"No," Marian said. "My orders are to do whatever it takes to get the job done."

"That's unreasonable," Trouble said. "What are you going to do now?"

Marian sighed. "Throw away my Space Patrol career, I guess."

"What does that mean?" Trouble asked.

"It means I'm going to try your idea, Miss Tate." Marian met Trouble's gaze, and said, "I'm going to disobey a direct order, and tell Mah'Ri the truth."

"Are you sure you want to disobey your orders, Marian?" Trouble asked. "Don't get me wrong, I think telling Mah'Ri the truth is the right thing to do. But Travis can tell you disobeying orders comes at a high price."

Marian appeared deep in thought for a moment, then nodded. "Yes, I'm sure this is the right course of action. I may pay a high price for it, but it will be worth it if the pirates end up paying a far higher price."

I felt Trouble's head bob. "If you're sure, then we're—"

In a flat tone, I asked, "Why?"

Marian's head jerked back in surprise. "Excuse me?"

"Why are you suddenly willing to disobey direct orders from your superiors? Up till now, when we pushed back on your orders, you always went back to your commander for new orders." I caught Marian's gaze and held it. "What's different this time?"

"I... Ah... I just spoke with my commander, and he didn't change my orders." Marian ground to a halt, broke my gaze, and then met it again with imploring eyes. "You must believe me."

"Must I?"

Trouble stirred next to me. "Why are you so suspicious, Travis?"

"Every good commander develops a gut feeling for a snow

job," I said. "And my gut tells me our guest is being less than truthful with us."

"I fully intend on telling Mah'Ri the truth about my mission," Marian insisted.

"I'm sure you do," I said. "But you also know I'm not questioning *what* you'll do. I'm questioning *why* you'll do it."

"I already gave you a reason," Marian said.

The intercom crackled, and Dave said, "Travis, did you notice how she worded her reply?"

"Yes," I said. "She gave *a* reason, not *the* reason."

"I wondered about her choice of words," Trouble said. "But I just assumed you'd flustered her."

"But not now?" I asked.

"No, not now," Trouble said.

Marian's gaze flicked back and forth between Trouble and me, then she sighed. "I told my commander this was a bad idea."

I waited in silence for her to continue. Trouble and Dave took their cue from me and also remained silent. Finally, Marian said, "SPIF gave me permission to tell Mah'Ri the truth. They don't like the idea, but they aren't willing to risk the entire mission over it." She paused, waiting for us to say something, I guess. When we didn't, she drew a deep breath, and continued. "I was ordered to claim otherwise, so I could be seen rebelling against orders."

"To make Travis trust you more, because you were putting your duty ahead of your orders?" Trouble asked.

"Yes," Marian said.

"That's just..." Trouble fumbled for words. "I don't know what it is."

"It's asinine," I growled.

"As usual, you're being too polite, Travis," Dave said. "You want me to set a course for the nearest Space Patrol station? If I push the *Lightning's Hand*, dumping our Spiffy guest will only cost us two or three hours' travel time."

Marian turned a stricken expression on me, and I thought it was the first genuine emotion she'd shown since we met. In a voice tight with unspoken emotion, she said, "No, you're my best chance to get permission to travel beyond Marsport's city limits. You have to take me with you."

"I don't have to do anything of the sort," I countered. "Especially since you've given us nothing but lies and evasions since you came aboard. Worse, you've done all of those things in response to orders you believed were... Let's be charitable and say they were misguided."

"What would you have had me do?" Marian asked. "We can't all have the same disregard for authority you have."

"You could try thinking for yourself," I said. "Isn't that something covert agents are supposed to be good at?"

Marian looked at the floor. "My training has concentrated on Martian lore and languages."

"Do you have any covert training?" I asked.

"Not a lot."

"Then why the hell should I take you with me?" I demanded. "Assuming Mah'Ri even wants me to travel outside of Marsport."

"Because you need me, Mr. Barrett."

"Do I? You still haven't given me a valid reason to let you tag along with me."

"The agent who infiltrated the *Bloodsword's* support crew is expecting a SPIF officer," Marian said. "You won't gain access to his inside knowledge without the proper contact procedures and code phrases. All of which, I know."

"I don't think we can trust her to tell the truth, Travis," Dave said over the intercom. "Besides, I bet we could pull this off without her help."

"Maybe we could, but she's right about one thing," I replied. "We'll have a much better chance of success with her help." I summoned my stern commanding officer glare and used it on Marian. "That's assuming she stops jerking us around and tells us the truth from now on."

"I swear I'm telling the truth," Marian said.

"You'd better be," I growled. "Because if I find out you've lied to us about anything else, I'll dump you faster than Dave dumps girls who fall in love with him."

Without a trace of humor in his voice, Dave said, "And I drop girls who do that so fast it would make your head spin."

"Is that clear?" I asked.

"Perfectly clear," Marian replied.

"Good." I paused for a moment, then said, "Did your Spiffy superior tell you to take command of the mission?"

"Of course," Marian said.

"Disabuse yourself of that idea right now," I said. "I'm in charge, and you will obey my orders without question."

"Now just a minute," Marian protested. "I'm the only active duty member of this team."

"But," Trouble said, "Travis is the only one with real-world command experience."

"It doesn't—"

I shook my head. "This is an accept-it-or-get-left-behind demand."

"It looks as if I don't have any other choice but to accept." Marian leaned back in her seat, tilted her head back, and sighed. "You're in command."

Then Marian rose, stalked into her cabin, and shut the door behind her.

trouble with redheads

A HUMORLESS LAUGH issued from the intercom, and Dave said, "That went really well, don't you think?"

"Shut up, Dave." I rose and turned towards Marian's cabin. "We really will benefit from Marian's help, so I'd better go unruffle her feathers."

Trouble blocked my way. "The last thing Marian needs is another speech from a commanding officer. She's had more than enough of those in the last few hours."

"I'm not her commanding officer." Trouble gave me an are-you-serious look when I said that, so I added, "But I see your point. I guess I can try a friendlier approach."

"God, why are men so clueless?" Trouble asked. "If I hadn't flat out told you I was in love with you, I'd still be waiting for you to figure it out, wouldn't I?"

"Absolutely," Dave said. "Travis probably understands the Mercurians better than he understands women."

Considering the solar system just learned Mercury supported sentient life a week ago, Dave's assessment of me struck me as extreme. But that didn't make him wrong. "Okay, how about giving me a clue how to proceed here?"

Trouble patted my cheek. "Pour yourself a drink and stay here. I'll go talk to Marian."

"Better yet," Dave said, "pour two drinks and bring one to me."

"You're piloting," I said.

"So?"

"Through the asteroid belt."

"Which we both know I can do blindfolded and with one hand tied behind my back."

Trouble raised an eyebrow. "Can he?"

I shrugged. "Probably."

"Then do it," she said, "and stay in the cockpit for a while. I might need to pour a drink or two for Marian, and that will be easier if you're not lurking in the lounge."

I nodded, grabbed two glasses and a bottle of scotch, then headed for the cockpit. Behind me, Trouble tapped on Marian's cabin door and called, "Marian? May I come in?"

I didn't hear Marian's reply, but her cabin door whooshed open as I entered the cockpit and dropped into the copilot's seat. A glance out of the viewport showed only two asteroids of any size, and the *Lightning's Hand* was well clear of their orbits. I poured the drinks and handed one to Dave.

I held up my shot glass and offered my traditional pre-mission toast. "To a successful mission."

Dave tapped my glass with his and offered his traditional response. "And to getting laid after."

We downed our drinks in a single gulp.

Having finally achieved some parity with Dave when it came to women, I couldn't help smirking. "How about getting laid during and after?"

"No one likes a braggart, Travis," Dave said.

"Says the guy who spent all his time in Space Patrol bragging about his sexual exploits."

"I haven't changed since then, either." A contemplative expression settled over Dave's face. After a moment, he said, "You know, Marian is about as tightly wound up as a woman can be. I bet the guy who gets her to unwind will be in for one hell of a ride." He grinned at me. "So to speak."

"I have enough problems as it is, Dave."

He waved away my objections. "You know I'd never do anything detrimental to a mission."

"That's good, because I'd hate to have to shoot my best friend because he accidentally sabotaged a mission."

Dave poured us another drink, raised his glass, and said, "To me not sabotaging the mission."

I clinked glasses. "And to you not getting laid during it."

Dave grimaced. "You expect me to drink to *that*?"

I threw back my shot of scotch. "Yep."

Dave studied his shot glass for a moment, shrugged, and tossed it back. "Okay."

We sat in companionable silence and watched the slow twirl of asteroids visible through the viewscreen. After twenty minutes, I heard Marian's door hiss open, followed by the sound of footsteps heading towards the cockpit. I turned as Trouble reached the hatch, extended a shot glass, and said, "Pour."

I did. She knocked back her shot, closed her eyes, and rubbed her temples.

"Problems?" I asked.

She nodded. "I have a better understanding of Marian, now."

Trouble extended her glass again. I refilled it, then prompted, "And?"

"Marian enrolled in the Patrol Academy with the expectation they'd train her as a pilot," Trouble said. "She has the aptitude for piloting, but apparently she also has the aptitude for covert work. Someone from SPIF met with her right after enrollment, told her about their secret Martian Traveller program, and recruited her into it."

Trouble shook her head in disgust. "They filled an eighteen-year-old girl's head with visions of vital work only *she* could do. Marian fell for their line, and she's been trying to live up to that sales pitch for the last five years. She's been doing everything by the book and following orders to the letter because she's afraid Earth's future relations with Mars rest entirely on her shoulders."

"Wait," I said, "are you saying Marian is only twenty-three?"

"I guess," Trouble said.

"Then how the hell did she earn a captaincy?" I asked. "I was twenty-seven when I got promoted to captain, and some officers thought *I* was promoted too fast."

"Oh, Marian mentioned that," Trouble said. "SPIF promoted her yesterday, after they heard about our trip to Mars. She said it's standard for people going undercover. Something about having a high enough rank that Patrollers and other military types will take her seriously, if she needs to call for military assistance."

"I busted my butt for five years just to make commander," Dave said, "and SPIF gifts her a captaincy one year out of the academy?"

Trouble shrugged. "Apparently."

"I obviously signed up for the wrong branch of the service," Dave muttered.

"Don't hold it against Marian," Trouble said. "She didn't ask for it."

"Fair enough," I said. "But what do you think I *should* do?"

"Just..." Trouble shrugged. "Treat her like a person, and not the great red-headed hope for humanity."

I tried my best to follow Trouble's advice, but Marian gave me little opportunity to do so. She stayed in her cabin for almost the entire trip to Mars. She emerged for good after the *Lightning's Hand* set down at Marsport's landing field. We left the ship fifteen minutes later. The Martians spotted our two red-heads, and Traveller mania engulfed the city.

LIKE TROUBLE and I had done when we smuggled ourselves to Mars a few weeks ago, I had hoped we could slip into Marsport and keep the redheads out of sight until we reached Mah'Ri's bar.

But Mars had other ideas. There are advantages to following the proper procedures after landing on Mars, but secrecy isn't one of them.

That went out the airlock when we reached customs, and it started on the Earther side of the process. The customs agent took one look at Trouble and Marian and said, "Those women aren't allowed beyond this point."

Fifty feet away, a stir rippled through the Martian customs agents. Within seconds, they stopped working and craned their necks to watch the drama playing out across the small no-man's-land separating the stations. Passengers clamored for the agents' attention, but the Martian agents' attention remained riveted on Trouble and Marian.

I ignored the commotion on the Martian side and slid our exit documentation on the counter to the customs agent. "I believe you'll find everything is in order."

He pushed the documents back without looking at them. "We got standing orders, bub. No redheads pass customs."

Like a hot potato from the children's game, I shoved our papers back to the agent. "If you'll examine the papers, you'll find they override your standing orders."

Irritation flashed across the Earther agent's face. He snatched the documents, snapped them open with a ridiculous flourish, and began reading. His brows drew down and his expression darkened as he read. Like many petty bureaucrats when they're thwarted, he made us stand and wait far longer than it took him to read everything.

After ten minutes, he handed the pages back to me and said, "Fine. Put your luggage on the counter so I can search it for contraband."

"Bahnt!" Dave's buzzer imitation further irritated the agent, even before Dave added, "Wrong again!"

I glanced at him. "You know you can be a real jerk sometimes?"

Dave turned a sad puppy dog eyes on me. "Only sometimes?"

I turned back to the customs agent. "Space Patrol pre-cleared our baggage, as it says in the orders you spent the last ten minutes reading."

The agent wouldn't meet my gaze. "I don't remember reading that. Give me back the papers so I can look for it."

I felt my temper slipping. "You read it. You remember it. Now follow the damned orders, pass us through customs, and tell us to enjoy our stay on Mars. Got it?"

"Oh, yeah?" the agent snarled. "I still gotta scan your Robosec's memory and storage."

The eyebrow lines on Rita's face screen slanted down. "There is no way I'm going to let you paw through *my* memories, buster!"

I vented a sigh of exasperation. "She's covered by the same pre-clearance."

The agent opened his mouth to protest, but Dave beat him to the punch. "Hey, Travis, did you hear they're looking for customs people on Mercury? What do you think? Can we get good ol'..." Dave read the agent's name tag. "...Jerry transferred to Twi-Town? I mean, Space Patrol owes you a favor or two."

I opened my mouth to play along with Dave, but the threat of Mercury did the trick. Jerry frantically waved us along. "I got people waiting behind you. Move along. Enjoy your stay on Mars."

We did as instructed and headed towards the Martian customs counter. Where a different welcome awaited us. Every customs agent on duty waited for us as we approached, and they all bowed when we stopped before them.

Still bowing, the senior agent said, "Welcome, Travellers!"

Trouble stepped in front of me, motioned for Marian to join her, and said, "Please rise. You honor us with your welcome."

The passengers waiting for Martian customs fell silent, perhaps struck dumb by the welcome the two women received. The agents rose, and the senior said, "It is you who honor us, Travellers." He waved towards a counter. "Please come with me."

The senior agent led us past the lines of people waiting for custom clearance, and that was too much for one man. "Hey, I've been waiting in this line for an hour. What makes them so special that they get to jump the line?"

At a glance from the senior agent, a junior customs agent went to the man. "Come with me."

The man smiled. "That's more like it."

The agent led him to a nearby interrogation room and motioned the man inside. As soon as the man passed through the door, the agent closed and locked the door. The man within pounded on the door, but the junior agent ignored it and returned to us. After that, you could almost hear a pin drop in at the Martian customs desk.

We cleared Martian customs and were bowed on our way in two minutes. But word of our arrival rushed ahead of us, and an excited, curious crowd of Martians waited outside the customs building. A cheer rose when Trouble and Marian stepped through the door. More alarmingly, the crowd surged towards us with excited cries.

I turned, shoved Trouble and Marian back inside the customs building, and closed the door behind us. To my relief, the door had a manual deadbolt on the inside. I shot it home just before the Martians outside began tugging on it.

"It wasn't like this the last time I was here," Trouble said. "What happened?"

"It's probably nothing more than bored people looking for a little excitement," I said. "We snuck past all these people last time, remember?"

"What do we do this time?" Marian asked.

As if on cue, the senior customs agent appeared. "Is there a problem, Travellers?"

Trouble raised an eyebrow. "Can't you hear the banging on the door?"

"You do not want to greet your people now that you've returned?" the agent asked.

"Listen to them," I said. "Do you think the Travellers can move safely through that crowd?"

The agent drew himself up. "Sir, no Martian would harm a Traveller!"

"Not on a purpose," I said, "but mobs can injure, and even kill, unintentionally."

The agent's posture wilted. "Of course. The safety of the Travellers is paramount. May I summon an aircar for you? It could land on the roof."

"Yes, please," Trouble said.

"Request a calm and discreet driver," I added.

"I'll see to it myself," the senior agent said. He waved to a junior agent. "Guide the Travellers and their companions to the rooftop landing area, and wait with them until an aircar arrives."

We waited on the roof in silence for five minutes before the aircar arrived. The driver bowed to Trouble and Marian, but made no more fuss over them. He and the customs agent helped the women into the car and loaded our luggage into the trunk while Dave, Rita, and I climbed in after the Travellers. The driver took his seat, piloted the car over the still-growing crowd, and headed for Marsport.

At my request, the driver landed next to the entrance to Mah'Ri's bar. Dave and I hustled the women out of the aircar and through the door as quickly as possible. I breathed a sigh of relief as the bar's door swung shut behind us.

Mah'Ri rose from the same table she'd occupied when we first met her several weeks ago. She nodded to Trouble, Rita, and me, raised a querying eyebrow at Dave, and then glowered at Marian. She jerked her head towards the bar's back office and stalked towards it.

"She doesn't look happy to see me," Marian said.

"Mah'Ri isn't happy to see anyone," Dave said. "But she'll be even less happy if we keep her waiting."

Without another word, we followed Mah'Ri.

Mah'Ri circled her desk and sat down. Dave and I leaned

against opposite walls, leaving the two seats for Trouble and Marian.

Mah'Ri leveled an appraising stare at Dave. "I'm surprised to see you again, Mr. Hayslett. You're looking..."

When Mah'Ri trailed off, Dave grinned and said, "Dashing? Debonair?"

"Sober."

"Ah." Dave's grin faded to a rueful smile. "I deserve that."

"Deserved. But no longer, I think." Mah'Ri looked at me. "It appears you have saved your friend, Mr. Barrett."

I shook my head. "You have it backwards. Dave saved me."

In a voice so low I almost couldn't hear it, Dave muttered, "Yeah, right."

"I've no doubt you believe that, Mr. Barrett." Mah'Ri folded her arms atop the desk, leaned forward, and fixed her gaze on Marian. "You only had one redhead with you last time, Mr. Barrett. Who is she?"

Marian said, "I'm Captain Marian—"

"I didn't ask you, child," Mah'Ri said. She glanced at me. "Well?"

"She's a member of SPIF—the Space Patrol Intelligence Force," I said. "For the last five years, SPIF has trained Captain Stark in Martian lore and culture, with an eye towards using the Martian obsession with Travellers to bypass Martian restrictions on Earther travel."

"She's a spy," Mah'Ri said.

It wasn't a question, but I said, "Yes."

Marian drew breath for a response, but I caught her eye and shook my head. Mah'Ri noted the byplay, raised one eyebrow, and asked, "Does she obey your orders, Mr. Barrett?"

"She will."

"What if she does not?"

"I'll abandon her to her own devices."

"Do you think you could do that, Mr. Barrett?"

"Yes. I would despise myself for it, but the stakes are too high."

"What makes you say that? I have not even told you what I want you to do."

"May I assume you've heard of the pirate ship *Bloodsword*?" Mah'Ri gave a single nod, and I continued, "A SPIF agent claims the pirates' base is on Mars. Specifically, in Kah'Freon, the state you represent on the Martian Council."

Mah'Ri's face remained as impassive as ever. "And you wish to hunt down and destroy the pirates who killed half your crew, destroyed your ship, and cost you your career?"

"I wish to discover the exact location of the *Bloodsword's* base, report it to Space Patrol, and let them destroy a murderous gang of cutthroats who have terrorized the inner system for far too long."

"How very noble of you, Mr. Barrett." Mah'Ri's gaze bored into mine. "And what of *my* case? Will you cast it aside in your quest for revenge against the *Bloodsword*?"

I met Mah'Ri's stare. "No. I gave you my word I would return for your job. It will be my top priority. But I *will* find the *Bloodsword's* base once I have resolved your problem."

"What?" Marian cried. "You can't do that, Mr. Barrett! The *Bloodsword* must be our top priority."

I shook my head. "I gave Mah'Ri my word."

Mah'Ri clapped her hands slowly. "An excellent performance, Mr. Barrett. How many times did you and Captain Stark rehearse this scene?"

I glared at Mah'Ri. "Three weeks ago, you gave me a spaceship in exchange for my word that I would return and perform a job for you. I have been true to my word."

"Thus far," Mah'Ri said.

"What makes you think I won't keep my word to the end?"

Mah'Ri nodded at Marian. "You brought her."

Trouble spoke for the first time. "That is why you should trust Travis *more*, not less."

Mah'Ri turned to Trouble. "Explain."

"Travis could have lied to you about Marian. He didn't do that. Travis could have simply left her on Carnegie Station and never mentioned the *Bloodsword* to you. He didn't do that, either." Anger ignited in Trouble's eyes. "Travis has given you no reason to doubt his intentions or his word. So stop pretending otherwise."

Mah'Ri met Trouble's glare for a moment, then her lips spread into a smile. "So, you fell in love with Mr. Barrett."

Trouble's glare faded. "Of course I did."

"Good." Mah'Ri turned back to me. "I believe you will honor your word, Mr. Barrett."

"I'm so relieved. Now, why don't you tell me what you want me to do?"

"How much do you know about Mars beyond the limits of Marsport?" Mah'Ri asked.

"Almost nothing," I said, "just like you Martians want it."

"Let's start with the short and simple version of our history. Martian culture peaked before your ancestors discovered how to create fire. Its decline began while humans huddled in caves and prayed to totems for protection from predators. Civilizations do not fall from such a pinnacle overnight, but the decline was obvious to all by the time Earthers began building pyramids. My ancestors pursued solutions without number, but never considered the one solution that might have saved us."

"Space travel," I said.

"Earth has a large moon, and it provides a nightly glowing reminder of what lay beyond your sky. Perhaps if Mars was similarly blessed..." Mah'Ri shrugged. "As physical frontiers vanish, cultures seek internal frontiers. Scientific and technological frontiers occupied our imaginations briefly, but few had the knowledge and training required to push those boundaries. Without real frontiers. We invented new ones. My ancestors' ever-inventive minds founded new religions, new political theories, and new philosophies. Adherents attacked those who didn't follow their particular belief, hastening our fall.

"Then, eighty years ago, you Earthers arrived in your gleaming spaceships, full of the vigor and arrogance and hopes of youth. Martians looked at you, and saw what we could have been had we but looked to the stars instead of towards our discontent. Many hated you for that. But your arrival fired the imaginations of the young of the time. They believed the solar system would be open to them." Mah'Ri snorted. "But the science and technology of ancient Mars fired Earther imaginations, and your ancestors wanted our wonders for themselves. Our leaders, whose pride the Earthers' arrival wounded, discovered renewed pride in our past. They refused any Earther trade proposal that involved our ancestors' discoveries. Those leaders established Marsport, and restricted Earthers to its borders. In retaliation, Earther leaders restricted Martians to Mars."

"Why didn't you just build your own spaceships?" Trouble asked.

"Our natural resources are long since depleted," Mah'Ri said, "and rediscovered pride in our past makes us unwilling to cannibalize cities that have stood for tens of thousands of years."

"This history lesson is fascinating," I said, "but I don't see how it helps us."

"I am coming to that, Mr. Barrett," Mah'Ri said. "Our decline has accelerated alarmingly since Earthers first contacted us, and Martian civilization is nearing the point of collapse. Governments still hold sway over cities and their surrounding towns. But warlords and criminal gangs control the outlying areas, and their control is expanding. Three small cities in Kah'Freon have fallen to warlords in the last two months. More cities would have fallen if the warlords and gangs didn't fight each other as often as they fight government forces.

"Kah'Freon's situation is dire, Mr. Barrett. Today's young look backwards to Mars' glorious past, and forward to Mars' bleak future. Disillusioned and easily swayed by talk of a return to glory, many leave the cities and join those besieging what remains of Martian civilization." Mah'Ri gave me a hard stare. "If those youths could venture off planet, they could put their yearning for glory to a good purpose. They could explore the solar system and open new frontiers. But conflicts between our governments and yours keep them confined to a dying world."

"I sympathize, Mah'Ri, but if you think *I* can get the Earther governments to lift their sanctions—"

"No, Mr. Barrett, those negotiations are for me and the representatives of Mars' other governments. But diplomatic solutions take time, and time is in short supply in Kah'Freon." She sighed. "My government's soldiers can not stand for much longer against the warlords' forces in battle."

"Why not?"

"Because someone is smuggling Earther weapons to the warlords. As their armories grow, so grows their boldness. If we could disrupt their illegal supply line, the tide of battle should turn back in our favor. But we cannot disrupt what we cannot find."

I looked at Marian. "Could the *Bloodsword's* crew be the source of these weapons?"

"SPIF hasn't heard anything about weapons smuggling," she replied, "but it's too much of a coincidence for the two to be unrelated."

I turned back to Mah'Ri. "Do you concur?"

"The young captain's conclusion is reasonable," Mah'Ri said.

"So," Dave said, "all we have to do is search war-torn lands, filled with people who look nothing like us, and find the most dangerous pirate gang in the solar system?"

"Succinctly put, Mr. Hayslett." Mah'Ri stood and pointed to her office door. "Come, we must procure your travel documents. You leave in the morning."

four
visa trouble

CONSIDERING MAH'RI'S POLITICAL POSITION, I thought getting permission to travel outside of Marsport would be easy, and I was right. As with Martian customs, business in the Martian State Department ground to a halt when Mah'Ri led Trouble and Marian into the office. The officer in charge assigned his most senior clerk to Marian and handled Trouble's visa personally.

That didn't sit well with a middle-aged Earth man in the waiting area. "See here, I've been waiting to speak with someone about my archaeological expedition for two weeks! Your continual delays force me to waste my dwindling budget on hotels and restaurants rather than pursuing vital research. But when two pretty girls slink into the office, everyone leaps to aid them?"

Dave smirked at me and sidled up to the archaeologist. "It's pretty ridiculous, isn't it?"

"It is indeed!"

"Maybe what you need is some pretty girls of your own."

"I beg your pardon?"

"Now that you know babes grease the bureaucratic wheels, you could always go to the Earth Embassy and hire a pair of beauties to grease your wheels."

The archaeologist turned a thoughtful expression towards Dave. "Do you think that would work?"

Dave pointed at me. "It's working for him."

"Perhaps," the archaeologist said. "But wouldn't those women have to travel with me?"

Dave shrugged. "So?"

"So... What would I do with a pair of pretty women at an archaeological site?"

Dave leaned towards the archaeologist and gave him a gentle elbow nudge. "The same thing you'd do with a pair of pretty girls anywhere else."

The archaeologist jerked upright, his cheeks reddened, and he waved a hand at Trouble and Marian. "Good God, man, I'd be old enough to be their father!"

"That's not a problem." Dave's smirk widened. "This far from home, I bet you can find any number of Earth girls looking for a father figure."

"That's enough, Dave." I pushed him away from the archaeologist. "He doesn't have much experience with polite society. Please accept my apologies on behalf of my friend." I extended my right hand. "Doctor...?"

The archaeologist shook my hand. "Harmon. James Harmon, representing the British Museum and the Smithsonian Institution."

"I'm Travis Barrett."

"Barrett? Barrett..." Dr. Harmon mused. "Where have I heard that name before?" Harmon's face brightened, and I steeled myself for a rehashing of the *Bloodsword's* destruction of my ship, the *Soteria*, six years ago. But he said, "Were you associated with that amazing discovery on Mercury last week? I'm certain I saw your name mentioned in a Smithsonian report."

"Only in passing." I didn't want to attract any more attention to myself than possible, so I changed the subject. "What are you doing on Mars, Dr. Harmon?"

"Trying, in vain so far, to get permission to travel to the *Umhos'ha Om'lu*."

From the corner of my eye, Mah'Ri turned an appraising eye on us. Taking a cue from her reaction, I asked, "That's in Kah'Freon, right?"

Harmon's eyebrows rose. "You're familiar with the solar system's longest and deepest canyon?"

I remembered reading something about such a canyon back at the Space Patrol Academy and racked my brain for its name. "Do you mean the... Um... Valles..."

"Valles Marineris is the Earther name for it," Harmon said. "But I prefer the Martian name. It's their canyon and we ought to respect their name for it."

"Quite right," I said. "Could you excuse me for a moment?"

I went to Mah'Ri, kept my voice low, and asked, "Is that canyon anywhere near where you want us to go?"

She nodded. "*Umhos'ha Om'lu* is twenty-five hundred of your miles long. It's near *everything* in Kah'Freon."

"An archaeological expedition would be excellent cover for our search for the *Bloodsword*. Can you intercede on Dr. Harmon's behalf and get an academic visa for him?"

"Yes, but it will take time." Mah'Ri glanced at Trouble. "Your lady love could probably sway the officials today by simply telling them that Mars must have brought Dr. Harmon here to help with her Traveller's Journey."

"Do you think that will work?"

"It's worth a try."

Clerks tried to stop me from interrupting Trouble and the senior official, but she heard our raised voices. "If my guardian wants to have a word with me, please let him through."

That was all it took to get a moment alone with her. I explained the situation, pointed out Dr. Harmon, and then returned to the waiting area. Thirty minutes later, a surprised Dr. Harmon found his expedition added to the two Travellers' travel documents.

The next morning, we boarded a canal boat and for our thirteen hundred mile journey to Kah'Freon and *Umhos'ha Om'lu.*

———

DR. HARMON HIRED porters to transport his equipment to the *Yamanzi*, the canal boat Mah'Ri hired to take us to Kah'Freon. She also had all our luggage transferred to the boat. She accompanied us to the dock, but stopped there.

"You're not coming with us?" Trouble asked.

Mah'Ri shook her head. "I wish I could, but the Martian Council's negotiations to open Mars to Earthers begin in the morning. I must attend."

"But how will we know where to start without a Martian's guidance?"

"I believe you will be better off without one."

Trouble's brows drew down. "I don't see how."

"You will look upon my world and my people with fresh eyes, and interpret what you see with a mind unencumbered by expectations."

Comprehension cleared Trouble's expression. "You think we'll notice things native Martians would miss because of their preconceptions?"

"I do," Mah'Ri said. "But I'm not quite abandoning you to your own devices. I'm sending you to a Kah'Freon Legion outpost on the border between the lands still under my government's control and that controlled by the various warlords."

I glanced at Trouble, and then back at Mah'Ri. "Are you sure we'll be safe?"

Mah'Ri gave a humorless laugh. "What you mean is, am I sure your woman will be safe?"

Trouble turned a searching expression on me. "Is that true, Travis?"

"Not... exactly."

"Don't start getting protective of me just because we're

sleeping together." Trouble sighed. "Did you think searching for the *Bloodsword* would be safe?"

"No, but—"

"And did you think finding the source of the weapons smuggling operation wouldn't be dangerous?"

"Of course not."

"Would you be worrying if Dave was your partner instead of me?" She raised her left eyebrow. "You *do* remember the office door on Carnegie Station? The one with TRAVIS & TROUBLE stenciled on it?"

"Yes, I remember. And... I'm sorry, Trouble. I'll try my best to keep my concerns at bay."

"You'd better," Trouble's lips spread into a wicked grin, "or your boast to Dave about getting laid during the mission won't come true."

"You, uh, heard that?"

Mah'Ri cackled at my discomfort and glanced at Trouble. "Men are so predictable, and so easily controlled." Her laughter subsided, and her gaze swung back to me. "Besides, the two women will be safer than you and Mr. Hayslett."

"Why?"

"It is our disillusioned youth—the ones most likely to rally to a warlord's banner—who most fully embrace the Traveller myth. Trapped on a dying world, they believe rebirth on another one is the only way they will ever leave Mars. They will die to protect Miss Tate and Captain Stark, and hope for rebirth on a better world."

"Okay..." I forced my mind back to our travel arrangements. "I assume you will contact the Legion outpost, and someone will meet us when we arrive?"

"I've already alerted Bangaz'Ri, the outpost's second-in-command. He will meet you when you arrive."

Trouble cocked her head. "His name ends the same way yours does, Mah'Ri."

"That is because he is my son. You may trust him with your secrets, and with your lives."

Porters carried the final two trunks of archaeological equipment on board. Dr. Harmon and his assistant, a graduate student named Andrew Baxter, who wore the resigned expression common to overworked and underpaid aides, followed the porters.

"We're finally on our way, eh, Baxter?" Harmon exclaimed in a jovial tone.

"Yes, sir," Baxter intoned.

"Inspect the cargo hold and make sure the porters properly stowed my equipment. It wouldn't do to go through all this rigamarole, only to fail in the field because of a transport mishap!"

"Yes, sir."

Baxter disappeared below as Harmon strode to the bow and struck a pose. I assume he wanted to look like an intrepid explorer braving the unknown in the furtherance of science. And if he was fifty pounds lighter and twenty years younger, he might have pulled it off.

I watched Harmon for a moment, turned to look at Mah'Ri, and sighed. "It's going to be an interesting trip."

She smirked. "Adding Dr. Harmon to the expedition was your idea, Mr. Barrett. Are you having second thoughts so soon?"

"I always have second thoughts at the start of a case. My qualms will ease once we're underway." I glanced back at Harmon. "I hope they will, anyway."

Trouble and I boarded the *Yamanzi*, the crew cast off, and the boat nosed its way from the harbor and into the canal. For good or ill, we were on our way.

———

TROUBLE and I stood together at the *Yamanzi's* stern and watched Marsport recede. Marian watched Harmon at the bow, then us at the stern, before disappearing down the passage that led to the passenger cabins. Dave watched Marian watch us, flashed a speculative grin at me, and followed the too-young Space Patrol captain.

I sighed. "I'd better go have a talk with Dave. The last thing we need is him upsetting Marian."

"Leave them to their own devices," Trouble said. "If Marian can't handle Dave—a guy who's about as subtle as an out-of-control ore freighter—without getting upset, it's best we find out now."

"What happened to that protective streak you showed towards her back on the *Lightning's Hand*?"

"It's a luxury we can't afford, so I left it on the ship. This trip will be filled with uncertainty and danger, and Marian will probably have to deal with more than her fair share of it. If she can't handle Dave, how will she handle the Traveller worshippers we'll meet in Kah'Freon?"

I considered her point. "You're right. But Marian seems so..."

"Innocent?"

"Yeah."

"In a lot of ways, I'm sure she is. But unless Marian's spent the last ten years living in a convent, she'll know how to deal with a man like Dave."

Three minutes later, Dave came back on deck, caught my eye, and shrugged.

"See?" Trouble asked.

"I bow to your expertise in this matter," I said.

"Good." She pushed off the stern railing. "Why don't we go to our cabin and unpack?"

Dave watched us go, and I couldn't resist flashing a lascivious grin at him. Without turning, Trouble said, "Stop that."

"Uh, stop what?"

"Implying you're about to get laid." Trouble glanced over her shoulder. "Because you're not."

"I didn't think I was. I just wanted *Dave* thinking about it. How did you even know what I was doing?"

"Men who think they're about to score adopt swaggering postures and mannerisms, and men who think another man is about to score adopt envious ones."

"And you saw that in Dave?"

"Yes."

"I'm impressed, Miss Private Investigator."

Unpacking only took a few minutes. I didn't get laid. Which is just as well, since someone knocked on our door just as we finished.

Harmon's aide, Andrew Baxter, called, "Mr. Barrett? Miss Tate?" I opened the door. Without waiting for a greeting, Baxter said, "Dr. Harmon requests you join him in the lounge for a celebratory toast, now that his expedition is finally underway."

"Sure, we'll be happy to," I said. "May I assume our companions are invited?"

Baxter's put-upon expression deepened. "Yes, but the other woman in your party refused without even opening her door."

"Go on to the lounge," Trouble said. "I'll get Marian."

Rita was sharing the cabin with Marian, so I said, "Rita should come, too."

"Don't worry, Travis, I'd never forget her."

Panic filled Baxter's eyes. "I didn't know you brought a third woman with you."

"Rita is my Robosec," I said.

"Oh, I see." Confusion replaced panic. "But your Robosec doesn't drink, does it?"

"No," Trouble said, sliding past Baxter, "but *she* socializes."

Baxter gave a distracted nod, turned around, and knocked on the door across the hall. I tapped him on the shoulder and said, "Unless Dave's moved in the last ten minutes, he's up on deck."

"Thank you," Baxter said, and strode off, presumably in search of Dave.

Behind me, Trouble called, "You shouldn't stay cooped up in your room, Marian. Come out and join us in the lounge."

Even muffled by the door, Marian's response carried to me. "No thank you, Miss Tate."

I went to Marian's door and called, "Rita, would you open the door, please?"

"I can't, Boss," Rita said. "Miss Stark blocked the door with her luggage, and my arms ain't made for moving enormous trunks like hers."

With a muttered curse, I banged the door with my fist. "Stark, open the door."

"No," she called.

"That wasn't a request." After five seconds of silence, I said, "Miss Stark, do you remember what I said I'd do if you didn't follow my orders?"

Five more seconds passed, and I raised my fist to bang on the door again. But the sound of luggage scraping along the floor came through the door. A moment later, Marian opened the door and looked at me. In a flat tone, she said, "The door is open. Are you satisfied?"

"No. You will join us in the lounge for a drink with Dr. Harmon and his aide."

Marian ignored Rita, bobbing impatiently next to her. "I don't want a drink."

"I don't care. You're still joining us." Marian crossed her arms and glared at me, so I tried a different approach. After glancing both directions down the corridor, I lowered my voice. "Miss Stark, I realize you don't like how this mission has begun, but you won't succeed at it if you stay in your room. Like him or not, Dr. Harmon and his expedition give us excellent excuses to search for clues to the *Bloodsword's* location. He's also far more knowledge-able about Martian culture and customs than any of us, which makes him a valuable asset."

She nodded. "I suppose you're right."

Marian emerged from the room, clearing the way for Rita. The Robosec stopped next to me and, in a low voice, said, "Good work, Boss. You're getting better at handling women folk."

Trouble smirked. "That's my influence."

The left eye on Rita's face screen shrank to a line and then opened again, imitating a wink. "I don't doubt that, Miss Boss."

I waved them after Marian. "Can we get a move on? I'm interested in hearing about Dr. Harmon's expedition."

Rita floated after Marian. "Seriously, Boss?"

"Seriously," I said as Trouble and I followed Rita. "Harmon might come across as a blowhard, but that doesn't mean we won't learn something from this gathering."

We learned something, all right. But it wasn't remotely close to anything I imagined I'd learn.

five
trouble with mythology

WE FOUND Dr. Harmon in one corner of the *Yamanzi's* lounge, reclining in an overstuffed chair. His chair, two equally-padded chairs, and a small sofa surrounded a low table, on which stood a bottle of Kentucky bourbon and glasses. Harmon smiled at us as Trouble and I settled onto the sofa, Rita hovered next to me, and Marian perched on the edge of one of the other chairs.

A moment later, Dave sauntered in with Baxter at his heels. Dave flopped into the remaining stuffed chair, eyed the bottle, and said, "You've got good taste, Doc."

"Thank you, Mr. Hayslett," Harmon said.

"My friends call me Dave," he gestured at the table, "and anyone serving me fifty-year-old bourbon is *definitely* my friend."

Harmon's responding laugh boomed over conversations, and brought the eyes of the other passengers our way. Our fellow lower-case-t travellers eyed us—the only Earthers aboard—with curiosity, and more than a few eyebrows rose when they spotted Trouble and Marian. I steeled myself for a rush of worshipful fans. Whispered comments rushed around the lounge, but that was all.

Harmon looked at Baxter, who had just settled onto an unpadded, straight-backed chair. "Why are you just sitting there, Baxter? Pour for our companions."

"Yes, sir," Baxter murmured.

He expertly poured two fingers of bourbon into each glass, and handed them around. Dave sniffed his appreciatively, while Marian took a cautious sip of hers. Harmon raised his glass and said, "A toast! To my new friends, whose generosity put my expedition back on track, and to a successful search!"

Since we hadn't told Harmon anything about our mission, I wondered what he was searching for. After taking a moment to appreciate the bourbon, I said, "We've been so busy preparing for departure that I never asked the purpose of your expedition. I know you're headed to *Umhos'ha Om'lu*—the Valles Marineris—but what are you looking for?"

Harmon's eyes lit. "Ah, therein lies a tale!"

"I hope you'll share this tale with us," Trouble said.

"As poor Baxter, who has heard this story countless times, can attest, I would love nothing better, my dear," Harmon said. "Right, Baxter?"

"Yes, sir."

Without prompting, Baxter splashed more bourbon into Harmon's glass, poured himself rather more than two fingers of the fine liquor, and offered it around to the rest of us. Dave took a refill, but the rest of us passed.

Harmon sipped, sighed, and began. "This is a tale of ancient Mars. A time when gods walked among men. A time of wonders. A time of legends." He leaned forward, his eyes glowing, and asked, "Have you heard of *Um'Vikeeli* and *Em'Toen*?"

Trouble, Dave, and I shook our heads. But Marian said, "The protector god and his wife, the goddess of beauty, I think? Their worshippers mostly lived in what is now Kah'Freon."

Harmon beamed at Marian. "Very good, young lady! Few beyond the stuffy halls of academia know of them."

Marian looked into her glass and swirled the remaining bourbon. "I've, um, taken some classes in Martian myths."

"Indeed?" Harmon said. "Did your studies include tales of *Um'Vikeeli's* and *Em'Toen's* daughter?"

Marian shook her head. "I didn't know they had a child together."

"They did, and upon her birth, both parents gave her a gift. *Em'Toen* bestowed the gift of beauty on her. Being a warrior, *Um'Vikeeli* gave her a sword he forged with his own hands. He named the sword *Insimbi'Vik*, the Protector's Blade. *Um'Vikeeli* and *Em'Toen* selected a name based on both gifts—*Umna'Enle*, which means 'beautiful guardian' in the ancient tongue.

"Our tale, and my expedition, deals with the sword. When *Um'Vikeeli* forged the blade, he imbued it with some of his godly essence. A warrior who wielded *Insimbi'Vik* in defense of his people would be well nigh unto invincible in battle. But only someone deemed worthy by *Umna'Enle* could use the blade, and that person had to receive it directly from her hand. Many thieves tried to steal *Insimbi'Vik*, and all died in agony.

"As you might guess, countless men sought *Umna'Enle's* blessing. They came from far and wide, initially interested only in the sword. But when they beheld her beauty, second only to her mother's, they sought her hand in marriage, as well. But *Em'Toen* warned her daughter against such a union. 'Love men and bed men, my daughter. But never wed one. For a mortal life is the price you will pay for a blessed union with a mortal man.'

"For many years, *Umna'Enle* took her mother's words to heart. She flitted from lover to lover, giving them neither her heart nor the blade, *Insimbi'Vik*. But there came a time when a vast, marauding horde approached her land, and the people begged their beautiful guardian to find a man worthy of the sword, a man who could defend their families and their homes.

"*Umna'Enle* relented. 'Send your bravest, mightiest warriors to me. I will choose the one who shows me the true heart of Mars. Three warriors answered her call, and she saw them one at a time in her throne room.

"*Kan'Zima*, the first to arrive, bowed low before the goddess, and offered a many-faceted heart made from a flawless diamond. 'By my own hand, I carved the Heart of Mars for you. Second to you in beauty. Second to me in hardness.' *Umna'Enle* took the diamond and bade *Kan'Zima* await her decision.

"*Thamb'Ile* arrived second. He bowed low before the goddess, and offered a heart made from the purest gold. 'By my own hand, I wrought the Heart of Mars for you. Second to your heart in purity. Second to my swordsmanship in skill.' *Umna'Enle* took the golden heart and bade *Thamb'Ile* await her decision.

"*Inli'Ziyo* arrived third, and last. With him traveled his grand-mothers, his parents, his two sisters, his brothers-in-law, and his nieces and nephews. He bowed low before the goddess and spread his arms wide. 'I appear as requested, goddess.' *Umna'Enle* looked at his empty hands. 'You bear no gift for me?' *Inli'Ziyo* dared to meet the goddesses gaze. 'You asked to be shown the heart of Mars, not for a gift.'

"*Umna'Enle* showed him the diamond heart. '*Kan'Zima's* beautiful Heart of Mars shows his hardness.' *Inli'Ziyo* nodded. 'It is as beautiful as it is hard, goddess. And as cold and uncaring.'

"*Umna'Enle* showed him the golden heart. '*Thamb'Ile's* pure gold Heart of Mars shows his skill.' *Inli'Ziyo* nodded. 'It is as pure as it is intricate, goddess. And as delicate and fragile.'

"*Umna'Enle* settled back on her throne. 'You disparage these gifts?' *Inli'Ziyo* shook his head. 'They are gifts fit for a goddess. But they are not the heart of Mars.' He turned and..."

Harmon paused his telling and his brow furrowed in concentration. "Blast, I always forget this next part. Baxter, do you remember?"

A soft voice spoke. "*Inli'Ziyo* spread his arms wide, encompassing all who accompanied him into *Umna'Enle's* audience chamber. 'The heart of Mars cannot be carved from a diamond or wrought from gold. It is too grand for such trinkets. The greatest artisans and most skillful craftsmen struggle to capture the merest hint of its beauty and intricacy, and most fail. Because the heart of Mars is not a thing to be captured. My family is the heart of Mars. My friends are the heart of Mars. My people are the heart of Mars.'

"*Inli'Ziyo* faced the goddess again. 'You are the heart of Mars. Even I, your humble servant, am the heart of Mars.' And *Umna'Enle* was filled with wonder at *Inli'Ziyo's* insight and wisdom. She rose from her throne and fastened *Insimbi'Vik* onto his belt. 'Shield my people with your wisdom and protect them with my blade.'"

Marian fell silent. Her eyes darted around our group and then fastened on her glass. She brought it to her lips and drained the bourbon in a single gulp.

"Hmph." Harmon glared at Marian, obviously annoyed that she had stolen his thunder. "You said you'd never heard that story."

"I haven't," Marian said.

"Then how did you know what *Umna'Enle* said to *Inli'Ziyo*?" Harmon demanded.

"Because I..." Marian lifted panic-stricken eyes to Trouble and me. In a hushed voice, she said, "I think I was there."

TROUBLE LEANED across the small table, took Marian's hand, and squeezed it.

Dave and I gave Marian sympathetic looks.

Harmon waved a dismissive hand. "Balderdash, right Baxter?"

Baxter downed the rest of his bourbon. "What, sir?"

"Why, I've given the lecture on *Umna'Enle* and *Inli'Ziyo* dozens of times. Miss Stark has never attended a single one, and I have an excellent memory for my former students. Isn't that right, Baxter?"

Baxter nodded and, in a low voice, added, "Especially the pretty ones." He glanced at Harmon. "I don't think that's what Miss Stark means, sir."

"What?" Harmon's brows furrowed. "Oh, yes, I see. The tale of *Umna'Enle* and *Inli'Ziyo* is obscure, but hardly unknown. Miss

Stark must be referring to whomever guided her studies into Martian Mythology."

"No, sir," Baxter said. "I believe you're missing the point."

"Quit beating around the bush, man," Harmon said. "What point?"

In a small voice, Marian said, "I'm a Traveller."

Harmon vented a vexed sigh. "I'm well aware of that, young lady. That odd Martian belief is the only reason my expedition is finally underway." He fixed a friendly smile on his face. "And don't think I'm not grateful to you and Miss Tate for your aid in this matter. For I truly am in your debt."

"Sir," Baxter began, "what I believe Miss Stark means is that she really *is* a Traveller. She remembered *Inli'Ziyo's* words to *Umna'Enle* because Miss Stark was present when he spoke them."

"Eh?" Harmon's eyebrows climbed towards his receding hairline. Then he surprised us all by guffawing. "I see, now! Yes, very good Miss Stark. Very convincing. If Miss Tate can act half as well as you, the pair of you will have the natives eating out eating out of your palms."

Trouble's gaze swung to the archaeologist. "Dr. Harmon, I—"

Baxter caught her attention, gave her a look that said *give it up*, and shook his head. Trouble gave a microscopic nod and changed tack. "I, um, get the idea there's more to the story? Surely, you didn't travel all this way to follow up on a tale you admitted is obscure, but not unknown."

Harmon smiled at her. "Very good, my dear, and very observant of you." He leaned forward and, in a conspiratorial whisper, said, "While perusing an obscure tome of Martian mythology, I found two words that sparked my interest."

"What were those two words?" Trouble asked.

"All in good time, Miss Tate." Harmon glanced at his aide and then turned a pointed stare on his empty glass. After Baxter refilled the glass, Harmon took a sip, reveling either in the fifty-year-old bourbon or our rapt attention. Finally, he said, "Galvanized to action, I spent the next five years scouring tomes unexamined since they were digitized half-a-century ago."

"You didn't examine the originals?" I asked.

"I did when convenient, or when I thought I'd found a passage that tied back to the two words that set me on my quest. But I finally pieced together the rest of *Umna'Enle's* and *Inli'Ziyo's* story."

Harmon paused for another sip of bourbon. Dave, never one to pass up the opportunity to steal thunder, said, "Let me guess. That *Inli* guy successfully defended what's-her-name's home and people from the rampaging horde. The beautiful goddess fell in love with him, ignored her mother's warning about the price of wedding a mortal and married *Inli*. I mean, that entire chain of events is kind of obvious from the setup, right?"

Harmon glowered at Dave. "You are correct, Mr. Hayslett. Though your recitation has none of the ancient grandeur found in the original tales."

Trouble gave Dave a brief glare, then tried soothing Harmon's wounded pride. "As Dave so inelegantly put it, we all knew *Umna'Enle's* and *Inli'Ziyo's* love was written in the stars. What we don't know is what *you* found. What tantalizing clue lay undiscovered for millennia, waiting for someone as knowledgeable as you to discover it."

"Succinctly and accurately put, my dear." Harmon lowered his voice again. "As you have guessed, the couple married soon after *Inli'Ziyo* defeated the horde. By all accounts, their love deepened with each passing year. They led their people, raised their children, doted on their grandchildren, and neither could imagine life without the other. But, in the passage of time, the curse of mortality caught up with *Umna'Enle*, and she died in *Inli'Ziyo's* arms.

"Grief overwhelmed the aging warrior. He belted *Insimbi'Vik* to his waist, lifted *Umna'Enle's* body, and bore her remains many miles across the plains, to the field on which he defeated the horde all those decades before. *Inli'Ziyo* laid her gently on the ground and drew *Insimbi'Vik*. He lifted his eyes to heavens, voiced a cry of unimaginable loss and heartbreak, and smote the plain with *Insimbi'Vik*. The force of his blow split the plains asunder.

"*Inli'Ziyo* built *Umna'Enle's* tomb within the vast canyon formed by his blow. The canyon Earthmen call Valles Marineris, and Martians call *Umhos'ha Om'lu*. But that is not the name *Inli'Ziyo* gave the canyon."

A soft voice spoke. "He called it *Isilonda Sosizi*. Grief's Wound."

I turned wide eyes on Trouble, but saw no panic in her eyes. Her lips spread in a gentle smile, and she said, "I think I was there, too."

━━

I TRIED WRAPPING my brain around the implications of Trouble's revelation. Marian's, too, but she wasn't my lover. Was Trouble more than the gorgeous, twenty-five-year-old woman sitting next to me? Had her soul animated bodies for time immemorial? How many—

Knuckles rapped lightly on my head, and Trouble asked, "Hey, are you still in there, Travis?"

I gave myself a mental shake. "What?"

"You totally zoned out." Concern lit Trouble's eyes. "Are you okay?"

"Me?" I gave a short laugh. "You're the one with the million-year-old memories."

"It's... disconcerting, as I think Marian will agree." Marian's head bobbed, then Trouble said. "But there's also something... Reassuring isn't quite the word I want, but it's close enough."

I thought Marian's eyes were open as wide as humanly possible. She proved me wrong by opening hers even wider, and asked, "What about this is remotely reassuring?"

"Well, you and I know that death isn't an end to life. It's just a transition to a new life. And it means I have more than one lifetime to spend with Travis." Trouble looked into my eyes. "Maybe we've already spent a thousand lifetimes together and have thousands more to look forward to." Trouble turned her gaze back to Marian. "How could that *not* be reassuring?"

Harmon had been silent since Trouble's revelation, his brows furrowed in thought. But his expression suddenly cleared, and his laugh boomed throughout the lounge. "By God, you young ladies had me going for a moment there!"

Marian turned a puzzled look on Harmon. "What do you mean?"

"The joke, Miss Stark." He gave a knowing wink. "It took me a moment, but I figured it out."

"What joke?"

"There's no need to keep up the act, Miss Stark." Harmon turned to Baxter and slapped him on the back. "Quite an amusing jest, Baxter. I'll be honest, I didn't think you had the wit, but you've proven me wrong." Harmon shook his head. "Travellers, indeed. Ha! I say again, ha!"

"Uh," Baxter said, "I don't think—"

As best I could tell, none of the Martians in the lounge noticed Marian's and Trouble's revelations. *Possible* revelations, my private investigator's brain insisted. But I wanted to get behind closed doors before we discussed them further. I caught Baxter's eye and gave a small shake of my head.

Despite Harmon's comments on his aide's wit, Baxter caught my meaning and backtracked his words. "That is, I didn't think you'd catch on so quickly, sir."

"You have to get up pretty early in the morning to put one over on me, Baxter. I assume you coached the ladies when you delivered my invitation to join me for a drink? You and I *are* the only people who know about Grief's Wound, after all."

"Um, yes, sir. That's exactly it, sir."

Harmon bestowed a broad smile on Marian and Trouble. "I must say, I wish my students were as quick a study as you two.

They take at least a week to learn proper pronunciation of Martian names."

"Thank you, Dr. Harmon," Trouble said. "May I ask what gave us away?"

"It was that folderol about spending lifetimes together." Harmon glanced at Baxter. "I would have expected something better from you than such romantic rot."

"That wasn't Mr. Baxter's idea," Trouble said. "I, uh, ad libbed that part."

Harmon gave a paternal nod. "Ah, well, I suppose I can see how such a romantic notion appeals to the female mind."

"Are you suggesting romance doesn't appeal to the male mind?" Trouble asked. "I'll bet the romance of the past is what attracted you to archaeology in the first place."

"Why, I suppose you're right, Miss Tate." Harmon's eyes softened. "That's quite an astute observation for one so young."

"It's nothing." Trouble waved a dismissive hand. "Just the accumulated wisdom of a thousand thousand lifetimes."

I still wanted to hear more about Dr. Harmon's expedition. "On the topic of archaeology, may I assume there's more to your tale than the myths you recounted?"

Harmon's eyebrows shot up. "We got rather distracted with that Traveller nonsense, didn't we? Now, where was I...?"

"You'd just told us how *Inli'Ziyo* created the Valles Marineris by plunging his sword into the ground," I said.

"Oh, yes. Well, there's not really much to tell after that, Mr. Barrett. *Inli'Ziyo* built a tomb for *Umna'Enle* somewhere in the canyon and laid her to rest within. He found himself unwilling to carry her sword any longer, so laid *Insimbi'Vik* on her chest and sealed the tomb."

"So you're searching for the last resting place of *Umna'Enle* and the sword?" I asked.

"Indeed, I am," Harmon said.

Dave swept us all with a mock glare. "All right, who left *magic sword quest* off my itinerary?"

"Relax, Mr. Hayslett," Dr. Harmon said. "*Insimbi'Vik* is just a sword, nothing more. Just as *Umna'Enle* is a woman, not a goddess made mortal. The tale I recounted is a fascinating story, but only a story."

"So, you're wasting time and money on a fairy tale?" Dave asked.

"Most of these tales have a basis in fact, Mr. Hayslett," Harmon replied. "I've no doubt a barbarian horde attacked an ancient kingdom in what is now known as Kah'Freon, and the kingdom's mightiest warrior led its defense. No doubt the magical elements of the tale rose over hundreds of years, as generations of poets and bards embellished the tale in their retellings. But I believe a woman's tomb lies undiscovered in the canyon. And, should we find the tomb, we'll discover a sword clutched in her skeletal hands."

Marian shuddered at Harmon's description, which prompted Trouble to stand. As I rose to join her, she said, "We hardly got any sleep last night, and my female mind says it needs a nap. If you'll excuse us?"

Harmon stood and took the bottle, effectively ending our little gathering. "Of course, Miss Tate."

A moment later, Marian tried squeezing past us as I unlocked our cabin door. But Trouble caught Marian's arm and pulled her into our cabin. "We'd better talk, don't you think?"

"I'm fine," Marian insisted, but she followed Trouble meekly.

"No, you're not," I said. "You look lost. Not that I blame you."

Trouble settled cross-legged on the bed. Since she didn't release Marian's arm, the younger woman had no choice but to sit, as well. Trouble remained silent, probably marshaling her thoughts. To my surprise, Marian broke the silence. "This is all just a weird coincidence, right? I mean, I *must* have run across that story during my SPIF training as a Traveller." In a small voice, she added, "That makes sense, doesn't it?"

"It might for you," Trouble said. "But I've never studied

anything about Mars beyond the basics every school kid learns. I'd never even heard of the Valles Marineris until Travis told me about Dr. Harmon's expedition, much less Grief's Wound." Trouble shrugged. "Cling to that explanation for what happened, if you want to. I don't have that luxury. But," Trouble's gigawatt smile lit her face, "I'm okay with that. What I told you in the lounge—the stuff Dr. Harmon called *folderol*? I believe that with all my heart."

Marian considered Trouble's words for a moment. "And you think I should believe it, too?"

"Why not?" Trouble's voice dropped to a conspiratorial whisper. "After all, that would mean you have a soul mate somewhere in the solar system."

Confusion filled Marian's eyes. "I do?"

"Didn't you listen to yourself when you filled in the story's final details? If you were reborn, don't you think *Inli'Ziyo* was, too?"

Marian pulled back in surprise. "What are you talking about?"

"Isn't it obvious?"

"But..." Marian shook her head. "Have you looked in a mirror recently, Miss Tate? If anyone is the reborn daughter of the goddess of beauty, it's you!"

Trouble shook her head. "My memory came from after *Umna'Enle* died, so I couldn't have been her."

Marian considered that for a second. "I suppose... But I couldn't—"

"*Yes*, you could," Trouble said. "Marian, *you* were *Umna'Enle.*"

trouble with officers

MARIAN STARED into Trouble's eyes for a moment, then dropped her gaze to the deck. "But... I'm not beautiful."

There are times—*many* times—when a man shouldn't butt into a conversation between two women. My gut told me this wasn't one of those times. "Who the hell told you that?"

Wide, startled eyes turned my way, and Marian asked, "What?"

"You heard me," I said.

"Um, I don't know," Marian said. "But it was pretty clear to me by the time I was sixteen. Boys hung around the pretty girls, and they left me alone."

"Sixteen-year-old boys are idiots," I growled. "I know that from personal experience."

Marian's gaze returned to the floor, and she was silent for a moment. When she looked up, her expression was once again composed, controlled, and closed. "That's very kind of you to say, Mr. Barrett." She slid past me towards the door. "Now, if you'll excuse me?"

Marian opened the door and left without another word. Trouble slid an arm around me and squeezed. "Thanks for trying, Travis."

I returned her hug. "It pains me to admit it, but I think Dave is right about Marian."

Trouble's eyes flashed. "What, that she just needs to get properly laid?"

"No, that she's got herself wound up so tightly that it's almost impossible for her to consciously relax. Did you notice how different Marian looked after she had that flashback memory in the lounge? Her mind was so wrapped up with the idea that she really was an ancient Martian reborn that her expression and posture relaxed. She stayed that way until just now, when I complimented her looks in a roundabout way." I shook my head. "It was like a switch flipped. Her shoulders hunched and stiffened, her eyes narrowed, and her lips compressed."

"She raised her shields incredibly fast." Trouble slipped from my arms and kicked off her shoes. "But we came back here so I could take a nap. And I'll bet you could use one, too."

We slept for two hours.

Over the next two days, my group of four adjusted our schedules to fit the twenty-five-hour Martian day, studied the maps Harmon brought for his search for *Umna'Enle's* tomb, scoured the maps for likely pirate base locations, and simply enjoyed the Martian scenery. Perhaps the most unexpected part of that scenery was the herd of wild horses we saw on the second day of our trip. When we voiced our surprise, Harmon slipped easily into professorial mode.

"Horses are quite numerous on Mars. They thrive on the red grass of Mars and the planet's vast plains give them room to run. Also, there are few remaining Martian predators large enough to attack a horse." Dr. Harmon gave a knowing look. "That's the result of several hundred thousand years of civilization."

"But how did all those horses get here?" Trouble asked.

"A good question," Harmon said. "There were no restrictions on travel in the early days of Earth-Mars relations, but mechanized vehicles were expensive to transport and even more expensive to maintain."

"Couldn't Earth expeditions just buy Martian vehicles?" I asked.

"In theory, but what remained of the Martian transportation industry was already hard-pressed to keep up with Martian demand. That made native vehicles almost as expensive as Earth-imports."

His voice filled with incredulity, Dave asked, "And transporting *live* horses was cheaper?"

"Not at all." Harmon raised his right index finger. "But horse embryos and the machinery required to bring them to term are a different matter."

"And," Trouble said, "unlike vehicles, horses can make more horses."

Harmon beamed. "Go to the head of the class, Miss Tate."

"Didn't the Martians already have something like a horse?" I asked.

"Oh yes, but millennia of controlled breeding rendered those creatures unfit for survival in the wild." As an afterthought, Harmon added, "It helped that the barbarian tribes of the Martian plains fell in love with horses, and quickly made them part of their culture. They're much like the Cossacks of the Eurasian steppes, in some respects." Harmon cocked his head. "Or the Cossacks were much like the Martian barbarian tribes, since the Martians adopted their nomadic lifestyle several hundred thousand years before our ancestors domesticated the first horse."

Trouble glanced at me, grinned, and, in a quiet voice meant only for my ears, she said, "Maybe *his* ancestors. *Mine* were right here on Mars."

I rolled my eyes, showing I'd heard her. Then we wandered away from Harmon's ongoing lecture.

On the morning of the fourth day, the *Yamanzi* docked at a ramshackle canal town. A Martian man about my age met us as we debarked. He wore a uniform consisting of a dark blue coat over a red shirt and red pants. He bore a striking resemblance to Mah'Ri.

I approached and extended my hand. "Commander Bangaz'Ri, I assume?"

He nodded, took my hand, looked me up and down, and said, "You are Travis Barrett?"

"I am." I gestured to my companions behind me. "And these are Tina Tate, Marian Stark, Dave Hayslett, and Rita, our Robosec. The other two gentlemen are our chance companions, Dr. James Harmon and his aide, Andrew Baxter."

Bangaz'Ri greeted each in turn and then led us to an open wagon hitched behind four horses. He helped us load our luggage into the back, gave the women a hand up onto the wagon, took the reins, and set off at a trot.

"Please excuse my haste," Bangaz'Ri called over the creak of inadequate suspension, "but I wish to return to the fort before the midday meal, so I can introduce you to the captain."

"There's no need to hurry on our account," I said. "We can dine with the captain another time."

"You misunderstand my reasoning. Understandably so, since I have not yet explained it." Bangaz'Ri gave the reins a shake. "I wish to catch the captain before lunch, because that's the last time that he'll be sober until tomorrow morning."

Bangaz'Ri reined the horses to a walk when we entered the village. Pedestrian traffic imposed the more sedate pace, and that gave me a chance to look around. I spotted half-a-dozen saloons lining the village's main street, two of which had upper stories. Scantily clad Martian women lounged in half the windows in those upper stories, leaving no doubt as to their profession.

One woman spotted our wagon and called, "Hey, look, girls! It's Stiffy!"

Bangaz'Ri's already-straight posture stiffened even more. A fixed expression settled on his face, and he kept his attention on the road. From his response, I got the idea the woman's nickname for him came from his posture and attitude rather than... something else.

The woman's gaze shifted from Bangaz'Ri to us. She clapped her hands in apparent delight. "Look! Stiffy brought us some new customers!"

The woman in the next window said, "They're so pale! Are they exotic, or just weaklings?"

That proved too much for Dave, who eyed the two. "I can go all night, and would wear you out. *Both* of you!"

The first woman leaned out of her window and shook her barely constrained breasts. "Oh ho! You should put your money where your mouth is, Earther!"

Dave grinned. "I'd rather put my mouth where the money is, Martian!"

The woman laughed. "I will look forward to that." She cupped her breasts. "Ask for Issee'Fe, eh?"

"And Ehhu'Ka," the second called. "I must see if you can live up to your boast!"

A third woman joined in the fun. "I lay claim to the other Earther man!"

Ehhu'Ka snorted. "You lay anyone who can pay, Sha'Ye."

"Like you don't?" the third woman retorted.

Trouble looped her arm through mine. "This one is taken, ladies."

The wagon cleared the knot of pedestrians. Bangaz'Ri snapped the reins, and the horses broke into a trot again. Dave twisted to watch the waving, laughing prostitutes for a moment, then turned to me. "Got a date tonight, Travis."

Marian sniffed. "Really, Mr. Hayslett, it is not a date when you pay for it."

"Oh, yeah?" Dave drawled. "What do you call it when a man pays to take you to dinner and a show?"

"*That* is a date," Marian snapped. "*You* are just paying for..." She gave a disdainful wave of her hand. "You know."

Dave laughed. "Trust me, the guy hopes he's paying for *you know* when he takes a woman on a date. I'm just cutting out the boring parts and know the fun part is guaranteed."

"Hmph." Marian's cheeks reddened, and her mouth compressed to the familiar line.

"That's enough, Dave." I turned to Bangaz'Ri, whose posture and expression eased as the wagon rolled out of town, and asked, "How safe is the town at night?"

"Most of the town's business comes from the fort." He shrugged. "Soldiers being soldiers, there will be drunken brawls, but the men rarely draw weapons. The town's pickpockets will ply their trade, as will the woman. The men will test your companion's capacity for drink, and the upstairs women will test his capacity for carnality."

Dave leaned back, laced his hands behind his head, and gave a satisfied smile. "Military towns. God, I love 'em!"

"Men are disgusting," Marian said.

Rita patted Marian on the shoulder. "Now, dearie, don't judge all men based on Hayslett. It's true, *he's* disgusting, but the Boss is a prince among men." Her face screen simulated a wink. "If he wasn't, Miss Boss woulda shot him by now."

Marian's lips decompressed enough for them to quirk up in a brief smile. "Yes, Mr. Barrett displayed decorum. As did Commander Ri."

The commander glanced over his shoulder at Marian. "You may call me Ban, Miss Stark, especially when there are no soldiers present."

Marian's expression thawed by a few degrees. "Then you should call me Marian."

"You can call us all by our first names, except for me," Trouble said. "You should call me Trouble."

"Of which she is quite a lot," I murmured.

Trouble jabbed an elbow in my side. "I can still shoot you, Travis."

"You could," I said, "but then Dave would be in charge of the group. Do you want that?"

Trouble gave a pretend shudder. "No."

"Oooohhhh." Rita's vocorder held a revelatory tone. "*That's* why you keep Hayslett around, isn't it, Boss? He's like a walking, talking life insurance policy for you, 'cause nobody would want to kill you when they could kill him, instead!"

Harmon spoke for the first time, and his voice held a note of interest. "Is that true, Mr. Barrett?"

"No," Dave said.

"Nobody asked you," Rita said.

"Stop it, children!" I called. "No, Dr. Harmon, it's not true. As I suspect, you already knew."

"I come from academia, lad," Harmon said. "We have more than our share of supposed scholars who surround themselves with lesser lights, just so they appear all the brighter. Isn't that right, Baxter?"

"Yes, sir," Baxter intoned.

I briefly wondered if Harmon viewed his relationship with Baxter in the same manner he'd described? I felt certain that's how Baxter saw it, but I did not yet know if Baxter played the part of a lesser light or truly was one. Then we topped a low rise and saw the fort a quarter of a mile ahead of us. Practical concerns pushed thoughts of academic relationships from my mind.

I glanced at Ban. "You said the captain spends most of the day drunk?"

"A man after my own heart," Dave said.

"Not now, Dave," I said.

Ban sighed. "Yes, Captain Edaki'Ve imbibes his midday meal. By mid-afternoon, he is effectively incapable of performing his duties."

"How does he lead his troops into battle?" Marian asked.

"Battle?" Ban asked. "Who gave you the idea we ever have to fight?"

"Your mother," I said. "She told us of warlords and criminal gangs besieging and conquering towns and cities."

"She spoke truly, but we just drove through the only town in the area." Ban gave a bitter laugh. "There is nothing here worthy of a warlord's attention, Travis, nor valuable enough to attract bandits."

"Then why does your government waste money maintaining a garrison?"

"It is easier to post the Legion's worst officers and men here at *Kaba Udoti* than it would be to force them from the service."

I refrained from voicing the obvious next question, but Trouble is more forthright than I am. She asked, "Then why are *you* here, Ban?"

"I am here for the same reason as you," Ban said. "I put on an act worthy of assignment here and Mother pulled political strings to insure the Legion sent me here."

"To find out how Earther weapons are getting into the hands of the warlords' men?" I asked.

"Yes," Ban said.

"Even if it costs your career?" Trouble asked.

"Even so," Ban replied.

"You and Travis have a lot in common," Trouble said.

"So Mother said." The wagon entered the shadow of the fort's walls. "We will speak more on that subject later." Ban slowed the horses to a walk as we passed through the gate. "For now, welcome to *Kaba Udoti*."

As we entered the fort, I looked at the interior of our temporary home. I'm not sure what differences I expected from Martian military construction, but what I saw reminded me of illustrations of frontier forts from Earth's history. I quelled my disappointment by reminding myself there's only so much men can do with a defensive outpost. Four tall walls, one entrance with a heavy gate, and interior buildings for storing equipment and quartering humans and animals.

Trouble voiced my thoughts. "It looks like a set for a French Foreign Legion movie. Something like *Beau Geste*."

"I won't bother asking how someone like you knows about

pre-spaceflight films," Dave said. "But it's another reason why you're a perfect match for Travis."

I turned to Ban. "Why don't you have guards posted at the gate?"

"We do." He pointed to four men leaning against the inner wall, who watched us while passing a bottle between them. "They are on guard duty."

"We can wait if you want to reprimand them," I said.

"There is no point. The captain will not punish them." Ban's shoulders heaved in what I took to be a fatalistic shrug. "He does not back my authority as his second in command."

"Have you reported his appalling behavior to his superiors?" Marian asked.

"Our superiors expect nothing else from those they send here." A bitter smile spread across his lips. "Do you know what the English translation of *Kaba Udoti* is? Fort Garbage. And once the Legion tosses a man into this garbage heap of an outpost, it no longer cares what happens to him."

In a low tone, I asked, "Even if someone is smuggling Earther weapons through here?"

"The Legion commanders do not believe anyone stationed here can handle such an operation in secrecy."

"Perhaps not," Marian said, "but couldn't some of the men facilitate it?"

"My superiors do not believe it is likely." Ban repeated his shrug. "My mother and I disagree. That is why I am here."

Ban reined in outside a building in the fort's center. To my surprise, a man in a dirty uniform hurried over, took the reins from Ban, and asked, "Did you run them hard, sir?"

"Just a trot, corporal."

"Right, sir," the corporal replied. "I'll take care of 'em."

I watched the soldier lead the horses away. "He seems properly respectful."

"Don't let today's behavior fool you," Ban said. "He cares more for the horses than for his fellow men, and would have given me a tongue lashing if he felt I'd taxed the animals needlessly."

Ban led us into the building I assumed held the fort's command staff. Inside, a young officer sat behind a desk, working diligently on an Earther computer that looked almost as old as me. He jumped to his feet when he saw Ban, stood ramrod straight, and slapped his right arm across his chest, and said, "Welcome back, Commander Ri!"

Ban returned the salute with less enthusiasm. "As you were, Lieutenant Nu."

Nu held his salute. "Have you given the civilians their orientation briefing, sir?"

"Not yet, Nu. I'll do so after they meet with the captain."

Nu frowned. "I am compelled to remind the commander that civilians must receive the briefing before they may enter restricted areas, such as the captain's office."

Ban sighed. "I know the regulations, Nu. I also know that if I waste time with the orientation, the captain will no longer be sober enough to meet with them."

Nu's frown deepened. "The captain's breach of regulations does not excuse yours, Commander Ri. If you pursue this course of action, I will be forced to report your disregard for regulations."

"Do as you see fit, Nu." Ban led us past the lieutenant and into a short hallway with a single door at the end. "Nu, as you might guess, is one of those rare men who obeys every regulation to the letter. He can be rather amusing in a pathetic way, when his guiding regulations prove contradictory."

"I heard that, sir, and will add it to my report," Nu called.

"Do as you see fit, Nu," Ban said.

In a disapproving tone of voice, Nu replied, "I will do as the regulations require, sir."

"Wow," Dave said, "I've met robots with more flexible minds than that guy."

"Watch it, Hayslett!" Rita's mouth thinned to a line on her

face screen, and the edges turned downward. "I'll have you know that my programming is—"

"Not the time, people," I snapped.

The mouth line of Rita's screen reversed itself. "Aw, you think of me as a person. That's sweet, Boss!" Her eyes cut to Dave. "But why do you think Hayslett is a person, too?"

Ban watched the interplay with an impassive expression. He knocked twice on the door at the end of the hall, opened it, and led us into an office about fifteen feet deep and twice as wide. A fat, middle-aged Martian man slouched behind a desk. I looked for physical signs common to alcoholics, but the red Martian skin hid the telltale signs of over-dilated capillaries in the nose and cheeks and yellowing of the skin.

"You're not my lunch," the captain said, his tone irritable.

"No, sir," Ban said. He gestured to Trouble and Marian. "These are the two Travellers I told you about, Tina Tate and Marian Stark."

The captain ignored us and craned his neck and looked down the hall. He raised his voice and called, "Where's my lunch?"

Ban turned to us. "This is Captain Edaki'Ve, commander of *Kaba Udoti*."

Lieutenant Nu called, "The fort commander should eat in the mess with the men, sir."

"Shut up, Nu," Captain Ve snapped.

"I shall be forced to include this incident in my report, sir," Nu said.

"You do that, Nu," Ve said, "and you can take your report and shove it up your ass."

"You should tell Nu that's an order," Dave suggested.

"Eh?" Ve asked. His face brightened as Dave's words registered, and he called, "Lieutenant Nu, consider that an order!"

Nu was silent for two seconds, then said, "But sir—"

The door to the building opened, and a slovenly soldier entered carrying a tray holding a small plate of food, a glass, and a bottle. Ve brightened, and glanced at Ban. "I'm officially putting you in charge of our guests, Ri."

"Yes, sir," Ban replied.

As the soldier placed the tray on Ve's desk, Ve waved us away. "Dismissed. And shut the door when you leave."

The captain poured and knocked back his first drink before we filed into the hallway. I glimpsed relief on Captain Ve's face before Ban shut the door.

trouble with ambushes

BAN LED us to a single-story building next to the fort's command offices. "This is the officers' quarters. We only have one spare room, where the women will sleep. You men will have to bunk in my quarters. I'm afraid it will be crowded in there."

Under his breath, Baxter said, "It beats sleeping in a tent."

"What's that, Baxter?" Harmon asked.

"Nothing, sir," Baxter said. "I'm just... thinking about our expedition."

Harmon beamed. "Good lad!"

We deposited Trouble's and Marian's luggage in a spartan room, furnished only with a narrow bunk bed and a small desk. Dave looked around the room and glanced across the hall at Ban's equally sparse room. He grinned at me. "My deepest sympathies, old friend, but it appears the room arrangements will put a damper on your amorous activities." Dave buffed his nails on his shirt. "While I—"

"Will have to spend a lot of money to catch up with Travis," Trouble said.

Marian and Baxter blushed at Trouble's comment, Ban appeared discomforted by it, and Harmon's brows drew down in apparent confusion. But Dave raised his left eyebrow and said, "Do tell?"

"We had a cabin to ourselves on the canal boat," Trouble said. "Use your imagination."

Dave leered.

Trouble gave an exaggerated shudder. "On second thought, don't use your imagination."

"Too late," Dave said.

"Hey Boss," Rita said, "want me to change the subject?"

"Yes, please," I said.

Rita's head swiveled to face Ban. "Back in Marsport, the Martians went crazy when they spotted Miss Boss and Miss Stark. The ones on the boat were more restrained, but I saw they were real curious about a pair of Travellers. But nobody's given them a second look since you met us at the pier. Why not?"

"That's a good observation, Rita," I said. "And a good question."

"Thanks, Boss." She turned her gaze back to Ban. "Well?"

Ban paused, probably to gather his thoughts, then said, "This fort is where the Legion dumps its worst soldiers. So, the town only attracts the dregs of society—people who cannot succeed in civilized society." Ban shrugged. "Belief in Travellers requires hope and idealism, and those are luxuries people who end up here cannot afford."

Dave glanced at me. "My first case with you took us to the ass end of the solar system. And the second one has taken us to the ass end of Mars. When do we get to go somewhere fun?"

"When a client pays us to go there," I growled. "Now, if you're done complaining about the accommodations, perhaps we could have a planning session?"

"What is this about clients and cases?" Harmon looked from Trouble to Marian. "Did the two of you hire Mr. Barrett and Mr. Hayslett to escort and protect you on Mars?"

"Um, not exactly, Dr. Harmon," I said. "I'm a private investigator. Miss Tate is my business partner, and Miss Stark is actually Captain Stark of the Space Patrol Intelligence Force."

Harmon's eyebrows rose to what was left of his hairline.

"What on Earth...? I suppose I should amend that. What on *Mars* made you join my archaeological expedition?" A suspicious gleam appeared in Harmon's eyes. "Did that cretin, McIntosh, hire you to spy on me?"

"No," I said, "we don't even know who McIntosh is."

"That's just the sort of thing someone working for McIntosh would say!" Harmon spat.

"I believe they're telling the truth, sir," Baxter said.

"Why?" Harmon asked.

"Dr. McIntosh's budget is smaller than yours, sir, and you can only afford one assistant. There's no way McIntosh could afford to hire four people just to spy on you."

Harmon fixed Baxter with a glare. "And just how do *you* know so much about McIntosh's budget?"

Baxter's eyes dropped to the floor. "Because he, uh, tried to hire me away from you, sir. At a fraction of what you're paying me. I turned him down, naturally."

Harmon leaned forward. "And what would you have done if he'd offered more money than I'm paying you?"

"I'd have stayed with you, sir," Baxter said. "After all, you already had approval for your expedition."

Harmon opened his mouth to say more, but I spoke first. "If you'll give me a chance, I'll tell you what we're really doing, and why we added your expedition to ours."

"And you will speak only the truth?" Harmon asked.

"You have my word," I replied.

"Which is only worthwhile if you're a man of your word," Harmon said.

"That's one thing you can *always* count on from Travis," Dave said. "Trust me on that."

Harmon crossed his arms. "I'll withhold judgment until I hear what Mr. Barrett has to say."

"Fair enough," I said. "Have you ever heard of the pirate ship *Bloodsword*?"

I shared an abbreviated version of Dave's and my encounter

with the space pirates and had Marian share SPIF's intel on the pirate base. She didn't mention the agent working inside the base, which was a precaution I approved of. When we finished, Harmon said, "You hope to use my expedition to cover your search for the pirates?"

"That's correct," I said.

"And you never had any real interest in my search for *Umna'Emle's* tomb?"

"I find the subject fascinating, but unless finding the tomb helps us find the pirates..." I shrugged, and left the sentence uncompleted.

"Well, it appears you are a man of your word. A dishonest man would have told me the opposite of what you said." Harmon frowned. "I don't know. It sounds dangerous..."

"But," Baxter said, "nothing Dr. McIntosh *ever* does will top it, sir."

"You're right, Baxter!" A feral grin lit Harmon's face. "By God, Mr. Barrett, we're with you!"

▭

WE SPENT the rest of the day planning our search pattern for the *Bloodsword's* base. Dr. Harmon even contributed a surprisingly astute observation. "I believe we should concentrate our search at the locations Baxter and I have already marked on our maps."

"Yes, let's ignore the pirate base so you can win a competition with your academic rival." Marian's voice dripped with sarcasm. "I'm sure the *Bloodsword's* next victims will understand."

In a tone of mild rebuke, Harmon asked, "Have you ever seen an ancient Martian tomb, my dear?"

"What difference does that make?" she snapped.

"They're vast, multi-roomed constructions, and always feature a cavernous central chamber," Harmon replied.

That observation caught my attention. "Is the central

chamber large enough to hide a spaceship the size of the *Bloodsword*?"

"The central chambers in every tomb I've studied were at least five hundred yards long and a hundred wide," Harmon said. "Is that large enough to hide the pirate vessel?"

"It is," I said. "Thank you for the suggestion."

Harmon beamed. "I'm happy to have been of service."

Trouble caught Marian's eye, glanced from her to Harmon and back again, then raised her eyebrows. Marian caught her drift, faced Harmon, and said, "I apologize for my... impolite reaction to your suggestion, sir. It was uncalled for."

Harmon waved off her words. "That was your youth, and the passion that accompanies such youth, speaking. I've heard worse from students. Think nothing of it."

Later, during an early afternoon break from our planning sessions, I took Marian aside. "Can you contact the SPIF agent inside the base? He could save us a lot of time by simply telling us where the base is."

She shook her head. "The ground crew never goes outside the base, so he couldn't tell us much."

"How does he send and receive messages, then?"

"Our agent doesn't receive messages at all. The chance the pirates might intercept a broadcast is too great to risk it. He sends messages via emergency messenger drones he modifies and then installs on the *Bloodsword*. As I understand it, the ship's weapons' fire activates the drone's launch sequence, and then flies to the nearest SPIF base."

"That's a risky way to send messages," I said.

"Which is why the agent's messages are few."

"On our flight to Mars, you told us only you could contact the agent," I said. "That claim doesn't align with what you just told me."

Marian looked uncomfortable. "I can only contact him directly."

"You mean in person."

"Not... exactly."

"Explain."

"Once we find and infiltrate the base, I can establish and mark a message drop."

"Please tell me you won't mark it by painting a big X on the wall."

Marian sniffed. "Really, Travis, SPIF isn't stupid. I have several micro transmitters in my possession. Once activated, they broadcast a short range signal on a frequency so weak no one uses it for messages. Our agent has a receiver tuned to that frequency."

"Aren't your superiors worried the pirates will discover the transmitter and become suspicious of the agent?" She shook her head, and I asked, "Why?"

She offered a brittle smile. "Because it's Spiffy spy stuff, the kind you disparaged back on Carnegie Station."

"Spill the details, Marian."

"It's classified."

"I don't give a damn. I need to know how it works."

She hesitated, then said, "The receiver is implanted in our agent's skull."

My eyebrows rose in surprise. "I had no idea something like that was even possible."

"That's why it's classified."

I considered Marian's story for a moment. "I'm unimpressed by SPIF's planning. It'll be dangerous as hell just making contact with the agent."

Marian rallied to her organization's defense. "We normally have months to plan delicate operations like this one. But your mission to Mars, and Trouble's involvement, gave SPIF an opportunity my superiors couldn't ignore."

"Even if their lack of planning cost the life of the agents involved?"

She leaned in close to me. "Look me in the eye and tell me you wouldn't give your life to end the *Bloodsword's* reign of destruction?"

"You know I would."

"As would our agent in the pirates' base. As would I."

I didn't doubt Marian's convictions, I'd just have found them more believable if she'd had combat experience. That must have shown on my face, because Marian's expression hardened, and she asked, "What?"

"It's nothing."

"The hell you say." Her nostrils flared. "Tell me."

I shrugged. "You'll probably follow your training if we end up fighting for our lives—Space Patrol does a good job preparing us for the worst—but you can't know how you'll react in a firefight until you're in one. Dave and I know two academy grads who froze the first time blaster bolts started flying around them."

"I am perfectly capable of controlling my emotions."

I raised my hands in placation. "And odds are you'll be fine. Most Patrollers are. But no Patroller I know has had a first mission anywhere remotely as difficult as yours."

Marian wasn't mollified. "You don't seem overly concerned about *Trouble's* reaction to combat, and she hasn't had *any* Patrol training."

"No," I said, "but she's already been at my side in a life-and-death firefight, in the Twi-Line wastes on Mercury. I'd have died without her."

Marian's eyebrows arched. "I... didn't know."

"Now you do."

The others returned from their break, and Marian and I rejoined them. By dinner time, we had our initial search pattern planned. Ban left to gather the supplies we'd need, leaving the rest of us to our devices.

Dave glanced at his watch, which he'd adjusted to Martian time when we landed. "I'm going to town. Don't wait up."

Marian crossed her arms, glared at Dave, and then at me. "I can't believe you're just letting Hayslett go. His drunken ramblings could ruin my mission."

I turned a bland expression on Dave. "Are you going to ramble drunkenly, Dave?"

"No," he replied. "I have other plans."

"Which are?"

"Buy lots of drinks for soldiers. Switch saloons often. See who follows me but doesn't socialize with me." Dave turned his gaze on Marian. "Pretend I'm drunk while pumping the soldiers who are drunk for information."

Marian wasn't willing to let go of her outrage. "What about your so-called date with those... Those... women?"

"The whores?" Dave asked.

Marian blushed again, and her lips compressed to a line. But she nodded.

Dave smirked. "Why do you think I told you not to wait up?" He let his smirk fade. "A good lady of the evening knows more about what happens in a fort like this than many commanders. But it will take me a while to get them talking."

Marian's expression registered surprise. "You're just going to talk to them?"

"No, *that* would make them suspicious," Dave said. "I'd never get any information out of them."

"So, you'll... you know?" Marian asked.

Dave put his right hand over his heart and assumed a pious expression. "Yes, I will sacrifice my body for the sake of the mission."

Dave grinned. Marian snarled in frustration. Then Dave turned and sauntered from the room.

Trouble watched him leave. After the door shut, she said, "I hope nothing happens to him."

"Me, too," I said.

Harmon, who had watched the exchange between Dave and Marian with interest, said, "Perhaps you should go with him, Mr. Barrett, so you can watch each other's backs."

I shook my head. "Dave is unparalleled at two things; piloting and partying. I'd just cramp his style. He'll learn a lot more without me than with me."

Harmon glanced at Baxter. "You're still young, lad."

"I can't hold my liquor, sir." Baxter shook his head. "I *would* jeopardize the mission with the drunken ramblings Miss Stark feared from Mr. Hayslett."

"Don't worry, Dave can take care of himself," I said. "Let's get dinner and then get some sleep. We've got an early start in the morning."

Despite the confidence I voiced, I worried about Dave until I finally fell asleep.

I **AWOKE** to furious hammering on the door to the room we shared with Ban, accompanied by unintelligible shouts. I ignored my body's protests as I rose from the hard floor, and my eyes automatically cut to the pallet Dave laid out for himself the day before. It appeared unslept on.

As a precaution, I'd positioned my pallet closest to the door. I took two steps and yanked it open so quickly the Legionnaire pounding on the door almost hit me before he checked his flying fist.

"What happened?" I asked.

The Legionnaire looked past me and said, "You're needed at the gate, Commander Ri."

Ban finished pulling on his boots, stood, grabbed his coat and sword, and made for the door. As he stepped over Baxter's and Harmon's pallets, Ban asked, "What's the situation, Sergeant Ta?"

"There's an *amah'hashi* band approaching the gate," Ta replied.

"How many?"

"Eight."

The door across the hall opened a crack, and Trouble and Marian peered out.

Ban paused from buckling his sword belt around his waist and glared at Ta. "You woke me for *eight* warriors? How are they armed?"

Ta shrugged. "Lances. Swords." He glanced at me as I finished buckling my blaster belt around my waist. "They may have Earther weapons. The gray of dawn still covers us, so I cannot say for certain. But they have the Earther who went into town last night."

My heart leapt into my throat. "Is he alive?"

Ta ignored my question until Ban said, "Answer the man."

"Your companion sits astride a horse led by one of the *amah'hashi.*"

"So he's alive?"

Ta shrugged. "It seems so."

Ban pushed past Ta and headed for the stairs. Ta and I fell in behind him. The other door opened fully, and Trouble, Marian, and Rita hurried after us. We were halfway down the stairs when Harmon and Baxter clattered down the hall and joined our procession.

"Real *amah'hashi* at the gate!" Harmon sounded giddy. "Quite a stroke of luck, eh, Baxter?"

"Yes, sir." Baxter's voice held none of Harmon's excitement. "Just our luck."

I looked at Harmon over my shoulder. "Do you know much about these warriors?"

"Some," Harmon replied. "Do you remember when we spied the wild horses from the boat a few days ago? I mentioned barbarian tribes much like the Cossacks back on Earth? Those are the *amah'hashi.*"

Ban and Sergeant Ta broke into a jog when we exited the officers' quarters. A moment later, we hurried up the stairs to the parapet overlooking the gate. We had no trouble spotting the horses and warriors fifty yards from the gate. The *amah'hashi* wore loose shirts over equally loose pants. Pre-dawn light washed away most colors, but something about the *amah'hashi's* clothing made me think it would appear multi-colored in brighter light. The warriors sat silently on their horses, except for the one holding the reins to a horse carrying a swaying man. I recognized Dave in that saddle.

Our appearance spurred the warrior on foot forward. As the man held the reins of the horse carrying Dave, it followed docilely. He called, "You are the commander of this fort?"

"Second in command," Ban answered.

The man stopped walking. "I will only speak with the commander."

"He will not be fit for conversation for at least another two hours," Ban said. "You may wait there, if you wish, but you must release your chance companion to us now."

The man began walking towards the gate. "Gladly."

"Stop!" Ban called. "You may not approach the gate. Send the Earthman by himself."

"I cannot. The Earther is in no condition to walk and knows nothing of riding."

In a voice filled with disgust, Marian called, "Just how drunk is he?"

"He is not drunk. He has been beaten. And not by us."

I looked at Ban. "Please let him bring Dave to the gate so we can tend to him. I'd also like to talk to that man and find out what he knows about Dave's beating."

"We are not supposed to allow *amah'hashi* near the fort, but..." Ban hesitated for a moment, then called, "Leave your weapons with your companions, then you may enter the fort."

"Will I leave as I enter, unharmed and leading my horse?"

"You have my word," Ban said.

"You expect me to take the word of a soldier of *Kaba Udoti*?"

Ban glanced at me and, under his breath, said, "He has a good point. Our fort's reputation for dishonorable conduct is well earned."

I looked back at the man leading the horse. "You also have my word."

"Why should I accept your word, Earther?" The man shook his head. "I will bring your man to the gate, but I will not pass through it."

Trouble called, "What if I also guarantee your safety?"

A sliver of the sun rose above the horizon, and the bright light of morning bathed the parapet. Trouble, never one to miss an opportunity, tossed her head. Red hair flashed in the sunlight, and one of the *amah'hashi* gasped, "A Traveller!"

Marian stood unmoving until Trouble elbowed her in the ribs and said, "Toss your head so they'll notice your hair."

Marian did as prompted. Her move wasn't as effortless as Trouble's, but Marian's hair waved about her head and caught the morning light.

"Two Travellers!" a second *amah'hashi* cried.

The man leading Dave's horse flashed a broad smile. "I gladly accept the word of a Traveller."

He spent a moment divesting himself of half-a-dozen weapons, leaving them in the care of another rider, and then led Dave to the fort.

"Let them in," Ban called to the Legionnaires at the gate.

I hurried down the stairs and met Dave and his good Samaritan just inside the gate. "Do you know what happened to him?"

"Three or four men ambushed him on the road from town," the man replied. "My men and I heard the fight. The men beating your friend ran when they heard our horses approaching."

Ban caught up with me, took the reins, and led Dave towards the officers' quarters. "I'll have the surgeon examine him."

I caught the *amah'hashi's* eye and asked, "Would you recognize his attackers if you saw them again?"

"It was too dark for such details. But I can tell you one thing about them." The man let his gaze wander around the fort. "They wore Legion uniforms."

eight

trouble with umna'enle

I LET my gaze follow the *amah'hashi's* gaze around the fort as I considered his words. Then I asked, "Are you certain you couldn't identify the men who attacked my friend? Even if they stood before you?"

The man shook his head. "Unlike your home world, mine is not blessed with a large moon to reflect light in the night. We discovered your friend as much by sound as by sight."

I'd only experienced a few nights on Mars, and those surrounded by artificial lighting, but I'd noticed the deep black of the night that lay beyond those tiny pools of illumination. "I'm grateful your travels brought you close enough to hear the ambush, and doubly grateful you intervened." I raised both hands with fingers spread—what Harmon called the Martian version of a handshake—and said, "I'm Travis Barrett. Please call me Travis."

The man mirrored my gesture. "My name is Isseehu'Lu, *ukateni* of the *Inlizyo ka Bomvu*. You may call me Hu, if you wish."

Trouble and the rest of my friends trailed after Ban and the horse carrying Dave. Hu and I joined the procession as I sifted through what little Martian I picked up from Harmon and Marian on the canal boat. "That's a... captain?"

Hu grinned. "It is."

"And the *Inli...* something *ka... Bomvu*?" I asked. "The army of Mars, maybe?"

"We are an army, friend Travis," Hu said, "but *Inlizyo* is the heart."

My own heart skipped a beat at Hu's words. "That's an interesting name for an army."

Hu shrugged. "The men chose the name, but it is appropriate, as our goal is not conquest but a return to the glory of our ancient ancestors."

I took a small gamble, and asked, "Ancestors such as *Inli'Ziyo*?"

Hu stared at me, surprise written plainly on his face. "You know of him?"

"And *Umna'Enle*, but I only learned of them a few days ago. From one of our companions, an archaeologist named James Harmon." I took a much bigger gamble and added, "And from the two Travellers under my protection."

Hu stopped walking. "You do not jest with me, Travis?"

I didn't stop, forcing Hu to catch up with me. "No, I'm not joking. You may speak with the Travellers once we're sure our friend is okay."

Hu nodded. "Thank you. May I wait with you?"

"You've earned that right. Dave wouldn't be here if it wasn't for you."

Ban stopped outside the command building, and I hurried forward to help him lower Dave from the saddle. My friend looked worse up close than he had atop the horse, but he showed me a cracked-lip grin. "You should see the other guys."

"Did *you* see them?" I asked as we led him inside.

"You mean, can I identify them?" I nodded, and he added, "Not from the fight. They had kerchiefs over their faces."

"Damn. But if you gave as good as you got, they'll be the only ones with bruised faces and scraped knuckles."

Dave shook his head, winced, and said, "Ow. Gonna be lots of bruises and scrapes, because someone started a big ol' brawl in one of the saloons last night."

"You think your attackers started it to cover their later ambush?"

"Maybe. Or maybe they hoped someone else would do their dirty work," Dave said. "Doesn't much matter which."

A haunted-faced, haggard, older Martian man staggered into the command building and stumbled to a side office. Without looking back, he muttered, "Bring 'im this way."

I glared at Ban. "Is your doctor another alcoholic?"

"No, he's a drug addict." Ban shrugged apologetically. "He's better than no doctor, at all."

Ban and I carried Dave into the doctor's office. As we propped him up on an examining table, the doctor fumbled at a locked cabinet, finally got it open, and grabbed a bottle from a shelf. The doctor tilted his head back, took two swallows from the bottle, closed his eyes, and gave a relieved sigh. When he faced us, the haunted expression still lurked in his eyes, but it didn't dominate his face.

The doctor approached Dave and, without speaking, began examining him. As the doctor poked and prodded Dave's wounds, Dave gasped and winced and hissed. The doctor offered no professional platitudes, nor did he apologize for the discomfort his examination caused. The doctor applied what I assumed was a Martian antiseptic, eliciting more wordless expressions of pain and discomfort from Dave. Not once did an expression even remotely sympathetic cross the doctor's face.

Thirty minutes later, the doctor stopped working and looked at Ban. In a voice as expressionless as his face, the doctor said, "He should rest."

"He has no serious injuries?" I asked. "No concussion?"

"Did I say anything about those?" he asked.

"You didn't say anything at all."

"Exactly."

I cut my eyes to Ban, who just shrugged. But Dave asked, "Hey, what about sex, doc?"

"Only if you can afford it." The doctor collapsed into a chair in the room's corner, leaned his head against the wall, and closed his eyes. "Get out of my office."

As Ban and I helped Dave off the examining table, Dave said, "Great bedside manner, doc. I bet the men all love you."

Without moving or opening his eyes, the doctor said, "I care not what you or the men think of me."

Ban and I half-carried Dave back to our shared room, and put him in the bed. Hu tagged along with the rest of our group, and I saw no reason to stop him.

After we had Dave resting as comfortably as his wounds allowed, I faced my friends. "From now on, no one goes anywhere alone. And we go armed at all times."

"Lest a similar fate befall us all, could you tell us what led to this vicious pummeling?" Harmon asked.

I looked at Dave. "Got any guesses?"

"I don't need to guess. I got beaten up because I spent a lot of time talking about how Martian civilization was all but dead, and played up the dominance of Earth's civilization."

I glared at Dave. "You went out of your way to piss these people off?"

My glare slid right off Dave. "Stick with your strengths, I always say."

"But why would you do that, Dave?" Trouble asked.

Dave glanced at Hu. "I think we should keep this in the family, so to speak."

"Then I shall wait below, in the common room." Hu caught my eye. "Remember, I wish to speak with the Travellers before I leave."

We waited while Hu descended the stairs, then I closed the door and looked at Dave. "Well?"

"There are two kinds of arms smugglers," Dave said. "Greedy bastards and true believers. It takes work to flush out the greedy ones, but if you can piss off the true believers, they sometimes tip their hands."

"You were *trying* to get beaten up?" Marian asked.

"Yep." A smug expression settled over Dave's face. "It worked, too."

"Except for one tiny detail," I said. "You told me you couldn't identify your attackers."

Dave shook his head, winced, and said, "I told you I couldn't identify them from the fight."

"You mean you *can* identify your attackers?" I asked.

"It's circumstantial," Dave said, "but I know who attacked me."

My eyebrows rose in surprise. "You know who attacked?"

"Yep," Dave said.

"How?"

In response, Dave tapped his head with his right index finger. He must have hit one of the many welts covering his head, because he grimaced. "Ow."

Rita fed a sniff through her vocorder. "It's finally happened, Boss. That beating, combined with the strain of acting civilized, has finally short-circuited Hayslett's brain."

"Not the time, Rita," I said.

Trouble laid a hand on my arm. "It's just her way of showing concern for Dave."

The mouth on Rita's face screen opened and closed, but no sound came from her vocorder. Dave winced as his swollen lips spread into a grin, and said, "I think your girlfriend broke your Robosec, Travis."

"Enough with the jokes," I said. "Who beat you?"

"Remember those four soldiers who were supposed to be guarding the gate when we arrived yesterday?" Dave asked. "The ones passing the liquor bottle back and forth between themselves?"

Ban's attention sharpened. "What of them?"

"They're the ones who beat me up."

"What makes you so sure?" I asked.

"While lording Earth's superiority to Mars in all the bars, I paid attention to everyone around me. The four men took turns watching me, but they were some of the few faces I already knew. I didn't have any trouble picking them out of the crowd. Especially since they always sat alone, nursed a single drink, and glared at me when they thought I wasn't watching. Those four are also the whores' best customers." Dave glanced at Marian. "It took me a while to coax information from the two ladies I, um... patronized. They identified those four as the biggest spenders in the fort."

"As if they had a source of income besides their Legion pay?" I asked.

"Exactly as if."

"Good work, Dave."

"Aren't you being hasty, accepting his explanation for this, Mr. Barrett?" Marian asked.

"I don't think so."

"Have you considered the possibility that Mr. Hayslett somehow tipped his hand?" Marian asked. "Isn't it possible the four men ambushed him because they saw through his deception and divined our true mission?"

"How would they do that?" I asked.

"How should I know?" Marian snapped. "Perhaps he drank more than he intended. Or perhaps he inadvertently said something while in the..." Marian paused, visibly gathered herself, and plunged on. "In the throes of passion with those ladies of the evening."

Everyone in the room turned their gazes on Marian. Red blossomed on her cheeks and rose to color her face. She lowered her eyes and muttered, "It could happen." Marian's gaze darted to Trouble, and then dropped again. "So I've heard."

Dave rolled his eyes. "Just because you read it in some romance novel doesn't mean it's true." He closed his eyes and vented a sigh. "Every guy grows up fantasizing about spending the night with two girls, but the reality doesn't match the fantasy. It takes a lot of concentration to satisfy two women at one time, and that doesn't even count the effort of keeping their names straight." A thoughtful expression flitted across Dave's face. "That's one advantage to whores. They don't care what name you call them. But even with them, I spent a lot more time calculating than passion throeing."

Marian's expression tightened. "Really, Mr. Hayslett, must your responses be so graphic?"

"*You* brought it up, sister," Dave said. "And if you think that was graphic, you need to get out more."

"That's enough," I said. "We have far more important things to worry about than Dave's experience with a pair of prostitutes."

"You are correct, Travis," Ban said. "First, we must ascertain whether those four legionnaires returned to the fort. If they are assisting the smugglers and believe Dave is onto them, there's no chance they'd risk returning here."

"Can we check on them without tipping our hand?" I asked.

"Easily. They have gate guard duty again today." Ban glanced at a clock on the wall. "Their shift began eight minutes ago, so they should report to the gate in the next fifteen minutes."

"Is there a window that overlooks the gate?" Marian asked. "Or some other way we can watch the gate without appearing to watch it?"

"That's easy," I said. "Hu, the *amah'hashi* who brought Dave inside, wants to talk to you and Trouble. If you do that outside, I can play the Traveller guard and keep an eye on everything going on around us."

"I do not know what I could possibly say to the man," Marian said.

"Chances are, he'll ask us questions," Trouble said. "We just have to answer them."

"Get some rest, Dave." I led everyone else down the stairs. We found Hu waiting for us in the common room. "Here are the

Travellers, as promised. You don't mind speaking to them outside, do you?"

"I am an *amah'hashi*." Hu's eyes turned to the ceiling.. "I prefer having the sky above me."

Outside, Hu led the two women a short distance from us and began speaking in low tones. Ban and I watched the fort come alive as the sun rose higher. Ban nudged me eleven minutes later. I followed his gaze. The four men we'd seen at the gate the day before ambled across the fort's grounds, laughing and talking and already passing a bottle between them.

If Dave's instincts were right, we had our first lead to the *Bloodsword*.

I turned my attention away from our four weapons smuggling suspects, and back to Trouble and Marian talking with Hu, the *amah'hashi* captain. Through my peripheral vision, I realized Harmon had his eyes locked on the four men sauntering towards the gate. Harmon jumped as Baxter's elbow dug into his side.

Harmon turned a glare on his subordinate. "What the devil was that for?"

"Don't stare at the suspects, sir," Baxter said. "You'll make them suspicious."

"Eh? What do you mean?"

"Watch them as if they were students you suspected of cheating during an exam," Baxter said.

Harmon's glare faded, and a sly expression settled over his face. "Ah, yes, Baxter. The *subtle* approach. Watch them from the corner of the eye, wait for them to tip their hand, and then pounce on them like a tiger."

"Except we shouldn't confront them, sir," Baxter added. "Should we spot something suspicious, we should alert Travis or Ban."

Harmon gave a slow nod. "Good call, lad."

As Harmon's gaze wandered away from the four gate guards, I caught Baxter's eye and gave him a quick nod of thanks. He acknowledged it with a microscopic shrug. Then Hu gave a wordless cry of amazement, and eyes all around the compound turned towards him and our two redheads.

Hu faced Marian, bowed deeply, and held his bow. Marian blushed deep crimson, and her wild eyes darted from Hu to Trouble and then back to Hu. She waved frantically at the bowing man and whispered something to him. Hu straightened and faced Marian with an expression I can only describe as reverential awe. As everyone else in the fort returned to their tasks, Hu spoke urgently to the women for a moment. Then Trouble and Marian walked to us while Hu watched them.

"What was that all about?" I asked.

Marian glared at Trouble. "She told that man I'm Umna'Enle reborn."

Harmon smiled and shook his head in amusement. But Ban regarded Marian with curiosity and asked. "Are you?"

"No," Marian said.

"Probably," Trouble said.

Ban looked at me and raised one eyebrow. I gave him the short version of the scene on the canal boat, when Marian and Trouble remembered events that happened in the dim recesses of Mars' past. Ban gave my explanation serious consideration, which proved too much for Harmon.

"Come now, Travis," Harmon said, "you're leaving out the part where Baxter coached these young ladies as part of a joke he played on me."

"I... didn't coach them, sir," Baxter said.

"But you told me you did!" Harmon protested.

Baxter nodded at me. "I did so at Travis's wordless request. I believe he didn't want to make a scene."

"That's correct," I said.

Harmon looked back and forth between Baxter and me. "This is all part of yet another jest, isn't it?"

"No, sir," Baxter said.

Trouble face Harmon. "I'm sorry we deceived you, Dr. Harmon, but it seemed like the simplest approach at the time."

"Does that mean you truly remember Inli'Ziyo plunging Insimbi'Vik into the ground?" Harmon asked.

Trouble met Harmon's gaze. "Yes, but we can discuss that later." She turned to me. "Hu wants to take Marian and me to meet the leader of the Heart of Mars." Trouble glanced back at Hu. "Though from Hu's reverential tone when he speaks of the man, I don't think *leader* is the right word. What do you think, Marian?"

"Prophet, maybe?" Marian said.

"It doesn't matter what you call the man," Ban said. He looked at me. "Surely, you won't allow them to do this?"

In unison, Marian and Trouble folded their arms, glared at Ban, and said, "Allow?"

"I'm sure he didn't mean it that way." I gave Ban a significant look. "Right, Ban?"

The man caught on quickly. "Correct. My concern for your well-being led to a poor choice of words."

Marian's and Trouble's glares faded, and they uncrossed their arms. Ban sighed with relief, and said, "What I meant to say was taking time to visit with this leader or prophet or whatever you call him could be dangerous and slow progress on the search for the pirate lair."

"*Or*," Trouble said, "it could improve our chances of finding it quickly."

"While I find the prospect of visiting an *amah'hashi* band exciting," Harmon said, "I don't see how it will help us find Umna'Enle's tomb."

"Don't you think the search will go faster," Trouble said, "if we have the help of an army?"

trouble riding

HARMON OPENED and closed his mouth twice in response to Trouble's question. Then he punted it to me. "What do you think about Miss Tate's idea, Travis?"

I shrugged. "She's right. More searchers almost always make for a shorter search." I glanced at Hu, who watched us from twenty feet away. "But will the leader or prophet or whatever of the Heart of Mars put his army at risk to help us?"

"Let's ask him," Trouble said. She turned and waved for Hu to join us.

Hu approached, bowed to Marian and Trouble, and asked, "How may I be of service, Travellers?"

Trouble kept to our cover story. "We travel in the company of an esteemed archaeologist." Harmon beamed a wide smile at Trouble as she continued. "His research leads him to believe the tomb of Umna'Enle lies somewhere in..." Trouble glanced at Harmon. "I'm sorry. I don't remember the Martian name for the canyon."

Harmon said, "*Umhos'ha Om'lu.*"

Hu turned bright, inquiring eyes to Harmon. "Is this true? You know the location of Umna'Enle's tomb?"

Harmon shook his head. "I know *likely* locations. Twenty-three of them, to be exact. I believe we'll find the tomb at one of them, but they are many and over one hundred miles separate the nearest from the farthest."

"We planned on leaving this morning to begin searching," Trouble said, "but there are only half-a-dozen of us. The search could take many months."

Comprehension dawned on Hu. "You wish to enlist the Heart of Mars in your search?"

Trouble nodded. "Do you think your leader would agree to such a request?"

"I cannot speak for Umba'Zo." Hu glanced at Marian. "He leads the Inlizyo ka Bomvu—the Heart of Mars—but should she request his aid, I feel certain he will give it."

"You mean Marian, specifically?" I asked.

Hu shrugged. "He would probably help regardless of who asked, but no member of the Inlizyo ka Bomvu could refuse Umna'Enle's plea for aid in finding the final resting place of her original incarnation. Least of all Umba'Zo."

"And what if I'm *not* Umna'Enle reborn?" Marian asked. "It's not like we've offered any proof."

"That is for Umba'Zo to decide," Hu said.

"How could he possibly know?"

"That is not my tale to tell," Hu said.

"What will happen to us if he decides I'm *not* her?" Marian persisted.

"He will bid you farewell and good searching." Hu peered at Marin with curiosity. "Did you think he would slay you and bury your bodies in a shallow grave?"

Marian didn't meet Hu's gaze, but she gave a noncommittal shrug.

"For God's sake, Marian," I said, "are you *trying* to alienate Hu?"

"It is all right, Travis," Hu said. "Her suspicions do not offend me. Rather, they lead me to believe she truly is who her fellow Traveller says she is."

"Why?" Marian asked.

"From the time of her birth, men sought Umna'Enle's blessing and the gift of the sword, Insimbi'Vik, which would accompany her blessing. All who sought the sword did so for their gain, for conquest in the guise of defense. Of necessity, Umna'Enle viewed all who came to her with suspicion, lest she grant her blessing to one undeserving of it." Hu met Marian's gaze and smiled. "Though she granted her blessing to Inli'Ziyo, she still harbored suspicions against him. Suspicions he only allayed after his successful defense of her people."

Harmon, his eyes shining with academic interest, asked, "How did he do that, lad?"

"It was simple. Inli'Ziyo gave the sword back to Umna'Enle." Hu kept his gaze on Marian as he responded to Harmon's question. "That simple gesture erased Umna'Enle's suspicions and freed her to fall in love with him."

I'd half-forgotten Rita floated behind me, until she said, "Hey, Boss, once we're done with this case, let's never come back to Mars. All these myths and stories about people getting reborn are overheating my logic circuits."

"Mine, too," Trouble said, "and I'm right in the middle of it all."

"You don't have logic circuits, either, Miss Boss," Rita said. She turned to me. "I guess this means we're all going to see this Umba'Zo guy and his army?"

I shook my head. "It'll be at least a day before Dave's in any condition to travel." I glanced at the gate and the four legionnaires who ambushed Dave lolling in the shade of the interior wall. "Besides, someone has to keep an eye on our local suspects."

Rita's face screen brightened. "So we're gonna leave Hayslett here? That's a plan I can get behind, Boss!"

"Not just Dave," I said. "Someone has to stay and look after him."

"You mean me, don't you, Boss?" When I nodded, a plaintive tone entered Rita's vocorder. "But Hayslett's got a whole fort full of people to watch him. Why does he need me?"

"Because I need someone I can trust taking care of him. You also know what's going on, can help Dave watch our suspects, and can comm updates to me on a regular schedule."

Rita grumbled about her assignment for the next hour as the five of us accompanying Hu made preparations for departure. Ban returned Hu's horse to him, then faced the wrath of the fort's stable master and got horses for Trouble, Marian, Baxter, Harmon, and me. Rita gave a dejected wave as we rode through the gate, rejoined Hu's small band, and set off for the canyon Inli'Ziyo named Grief's Wound.

WHEN HU THOUGHT none of us were paying attention to him, he assigned one of his men to ride alongside each of us Earthers. He even assigned himself to ride with me, ostensibly so I could relate our tale to him. At first, he cast surreptitious glances my way as I told him of the *Soteria*, and of her destruction under the pounding of the *Bloodsword's* blaster cannons.

He listened somberly and, when I wound down, put his hand on my shoulder. "Ghosts are poor company at the best of times, Travis. But ghosts who cry out for justice? Their company is the hardest to bear."

"I... have grown used to their company, Hu," I said. "These days, I'm driven more by a desire to protect those who haven't yet crossed paths with the *Bloodsword*, but are destined to do so in the future."

Hu regarded me for a moment, then his mouth spread in a fierce smile. "You are the spiritual brother of Inli'Ziyo."

"As long as I'm not his *real* brother. I think we have enough Travellers already."

"Inli'Ziyo only had sisters, so that is one concern you may lay aside." Hu looked at Trouble. "Though it is possible *she* is one of his sisters, reborn. It would explain why she remembers the creation of Grief's Wound." He turned back to me. "Tell me of your meeting, and how you fell in love."

"It's a far happier tale than the *Soteria*, but Trouble tells it better than I do."

"She has the look of an animated and entertaining storyteller, but I wish to hear it from you first."

I gave Hu a wry look. "Is that because you want to hear the story, or because you're still evaluating how well I can ride?"

Hu laughed. "I had hoped my ploy was more subtle, Travis."

"You have a man riding close enough to grab the bridle from my companions if they lose control of their horses and are ready to do the same for me." I shook my head. "That's like waving a red flag for a private investigator like me."

Hu shrugged. "After I saw how poorly your friend, Dave, sat in the saddle, can you blame me?"

"He'd just been beaten."

"I took that into consideration."

It was my turn to shrug. "Dave is a pilot."

"Ah." Hu gave a slow nod of understanding. "He feels an empathic connection to machines rather than beasts, yes?"

"That could be the most succinct description of Dave I've ever heard."

"And you are his opposite, which explains why you and he are such great friends. But that doesn't explain where you learned to ride."

"I grew up on a farm."

"And your companions?"

I looked around. "Harmon and Baxter probably learned from necessity when working at remote archaeological digs. Marian has had the benefit of... atypical Space Patrol training. Riding was probably part of it." I looked at Trouble, who was chatting easily with the *amah'hashi* riding next to her. "I don't know where Trouble learned to ride. Her family is wealthy, and her father gave her money instead of love. But she grew up on Carnegie Station in the asteroid belt, which isn't a suitable environment for horses."

As if she sensed my attention on her, Trouble turned my way and grinned. "Are you talking about me?"

"We were just wondering where you learned to ride," I said.

"I learned on a simulator. It taught me how to ride, but riding a real horse is so much more exciting." She patted her horse's flank. "He speaks to me with body language, and I'm surprised how well I understand him."

Hu raised an eyebrow. "What is he telling you now?"

"He's telling me..." Trouble glanced at the man riding next to her. A mischievous spark lit her eyes when she realized he wasn't watching her as closely as before. She gave her horse a kick in the flanks. The horse surged into a gallop. "He wants to run!"

I'd seen the glint in Trouble's eyes, so her move didn't catch me by surprise. I gave my horse a kick, bent low in the saddle, and I chased after her. My horse and I slowly closed the gap until we were riding side by side with Trouble and her horse. A quick glance over my shoulder revealed the rest of the group strung out behind us, all galloping in pursuit.

Next to me, Trouble laughed for the sheer joy of the ride. I couldn't help laughing with her, as the specters of my past fell behind me. They always do so when Trouble makes me live in the moment, rather than dwelling in the past.

We charged up a small hill, neck and neck, racing to the top. We reined in there, but not because we were tired of the thrill of the ride and the wind on our faces. What we saw beyond the hill stopped us. *Umhos'ha Om'lu*, Valles Marineris to Earthers, Grief's Wound to Inli'Ziyo, lay before us. A scar in the ground that stretched as far as the eye could see, and whose depths disappeared in dark shadows.

Trouble gasped. "Oh, Travis, it's more beautiful than I remember."

I could think of nothing to say, so I took Trouble's hand in mine and gave it a gentle squeeze. The others thundered up beside us. The eight Martians with us were less moved by the sight than we Earthers. I guess even such unmatched grandeur must become commonplace after enough exposure.

Hu stopped next to me, and Marian stopped next to Trouble, and stared with rapidly blinking eyes at the canyon before us. Trouble laid her free hand on Marian's shoulder, and said, "It's a fitting monument to Umna'Enle, don't you think?"

Marian's blinking slowed, her mouth settled into its usual line, and she said, "It's just a big hole in the ground."

Trouble opened her mouth to say something, but one of Hu's men rode up to Hu and said, "Look behind us."

We all turned and looked back the way we had come. Hu stiffened next to me. I didn't see anything out of the ordinary, so asked, "What do you see?"

Hu pointed at something in the distance. "Dust from horses. Someone is following us."

I squinted into the glare from the morning sun and searched the horizon for the telltale dust Hu and his men saw. "Are you pointing at that reddish smudge that's low on the horizon?"

"Oh, I see it now," Trouble said. "But I don't know how the *amah'hashi* spotted it."

"We make our homes in the plains and deserts of Mars," Hu said, "and our survival rests on our ability to recognize those things that are out of place here."

Baxter spoke for the time since we had left the fort. "How do you know it's not simply the wind at work?"

"That is a good question," Hu said. "Dust storms on our world tend to be vast affairs that have swallowed entire tribes and left no trace behind. It is possible that the dust cloud is the precursor to a great storm. And whether it marks pursuers or a building storm, we should watch it."

Harmon gave a decisive nod. "That is a wise precaution."

We turned our horses and started down the side of the hill facing the gigantic canyon. Trouble kept her eyes on the ground ahead of her horse, but said, "Neither you nor your men think it's a storm, Hu. Could you explain why?"

"This terrain rarely births storms..." Hu paused. "How do you wish to be addressed by my men and I? I believe Miss Tate is a properly respectful form of address commonly used by Earthers. We could also address you as Lady Traveller." Hu looked at Marian. "We would use the same honorific for both of you."

Trouble laughed. "God, no, Hu. Discovering we are Travellers is weird enough without adding fancy titles to mix. No ladyships for me! My friends call me Trouble. You and your men should, too."

"Marian or Miss Stark are acceptable," Marian said.

"Now that we've settled that question," Trouble said, "you were in the middle of answering my question about the cloud of dust behind us."

Hu shrugged. "My answer is essentially complete. If the cloud does not mark a storm, it likely marks the movement of many animals."

"Such as the horses ridden by the *amah'hashi*," Trouble said.

"Exactly."

Trouble nodded. "So you and your men will watch the dust behind us. If it follows us, it's another tribe. And that's... bad?"

Hu shook his head. "The Heart of Mars has good relations with the other tribes in the area. It is those who usurp the name *amah'hashi* as a cover for conquest or criminal behavior who worry me."

"Ban warned us of warlords and marauding gangs," I said, "as did his mother before we left Marsport."

"What would the false *amah'hashi* do if they caught us?" Trouble asked.

"Kill my men and me and then take you Earthers prisoner. Idealistic young people would flock to any warlord who had two Travellers among his followers."

Marian sniffed. "What makes you think Miss Tate or I would cooperate with such a man?"

"Because he would torture your male companions if you did not." Hu lowered his voice. "If you refuse to do the warlord's bidding, he would torture the young academic to death as an example of his ruthlessness."

"Why Baxter?" Marian asked.

"The warlord would keep me around because Trouble loves me," I said, "and Harmon because he can help lead the warlord to Umna'Enle's tomb. In that light, Baxter only has value as an example to deter misbehavior."

"You speak truly, Travis," Hu said.

Marian glanced at Baxter, riding a dozen yards behind us. "That's barbaric."

"Collapsing civilizations always are," I said. "No offense, Hu."

"The truth cannot offend." Hu flashed a rueful smile. "Perhaps I should say, the truth *should* not offend. For I find your words, true though they be, distasteful."

"I'm sure I would feel the same, in your place," I said. "Meanwhile, what are your plans for evading our pursuers?"

"Since you have all shown yourselves to be capable riders, we will move faster."

"Can we reach your main camp before nightfall?" Marian asked.

"I wish we could," Hu said. "But if we set a fast enough pace, those following us will be unable to close the gap between us. That will have to do."

Hu called a command to his men and kicked his horse into a trot. The rest of us followed his lead, and our horses fell into the mile-eating pace natural to them. And while we didn't widen the distance to our pursuers, they didn't close the distance, either. Hu mixed brief rests and periods of walking, to keep the horses from exhausting themselves. But it exhausted us five Earthers, none of whom had ridden such a distance and at such a pace in our lives.

Hu didn't call a halt until the sun dipped low on the horizon. His men dismounted, tended to their horses, helped us tend to ours, and then set up the camp. One cooked a simple dinner, which we all ate with gusto.

Hu assigned a watch schedule and politely declined my offer to join. "My men and I know this land and its sounds. I appreciate your offer, but you will best help us if you get a full night's sleep."

I couldn't argue with his reasoning. With a nod acknowledging his point, I went to help Trouble and Marian lay out their sleeping pallets. I unrolled mine next to Trouble's, gave her a quick kiss, and then we crawled under our blankets. Trouble fell asleep immediately. A minute later, I followed her into dreamland.

ten
trouble with inli'ziyo

I WENT from the deepest sleep to wide awake in an instant. Trouble's soft breathing met my ears, as did the nearby, rhythmic breathing of Marian, Harmon, and Baxter. I heard no other sound, but a sixth sense warned me danger lurked nearby. From years of experience in the Space Patrol and as a private investigator, I knew better than to ignore its call.

No light flickered through my closed eyelids, so I risked opening them. Darkness blanketed the planet, so nearly total that I sensed more than saw Trouble sleeping beside me. I removed the blanket that covered me, taking care to not make a sound, shivered as the cold night air enveloped me, and sat up. I stared into the night, and the darkness gradually resolved into deep shadows and deeper shadows. Something moved near me, sensed rather than heard or seen.

Warm air blew across my right ear. In a voice so low I only heard it because of the unnatural silence, Hu said, "Remain silent, Travis, but wake your companions."

I nodded, trusting Hu was close enough to see it, and then leaned over Trouble and slid my hand over her mouth. She awakened with a start. I kept my voice as low as Hu had. "Something's up. Stay as quiet as possible, and wake Marian. I'll take care of Harmon and Baxter."

Trouble nodded, which I felt from my hand over her mouth, and began disentangling herself from her blanket. I crawled to Harmon and Baxter and took the same care waking them. To my surprise, Harmon didn't ply me with questions I couldn't answer. We felt our way back to Trouble and Marian. My sixth sense told me both women were alert and as ready for danger as possible, given the circumstances.

From beyond our small campsite, a torch flared to life. The flame's weak light seemed searingly bright in the dark Martian night. It silhouetted the man holding the torch and two dark forms on either side of him. Those two forms moved, and each lit a torch from the first one. Then men next to them lit torches from theirs. The ring of flame quickly surrounded us, the only sound coming from the burning torches' low crackling.

The twin lines of light converged directly opposite the man who lit the first torch and illuminated a man who held a sword rather than a torch. The man was cut from the same cloth as Hu and the other *amah'hashi*; lean, and dressed in the same loose clothing. Without a word, he swept his sword into an intricate series of cuts and slashes. The blade became a flashing blur as it slashed the air.

The man raised the blade high, reversed it with a flick of his wrist, and drove the point into the ground before him. "I am Isih'Luku, om'ukateni of the Isifith'Ifithi."

"What's happening?" Marian asked.

Hu raised a hand to Marian, requesting silence. "Isih'Luku, may I have a moment to explain our traditions to the Earthers? It is best they understand their part in this before we begin."

Isih'Luku considered Hu's request for a moment. "You may."

Hu brought us in close and kept his voice low. "This is an ancient tradition among the *amah'hashi*. It's a challenge to single combat between leaders."

"Meaning he challenged you," I said.

Hu nodded. "If I defeat Isih'Luku, his men will abandon their property, including horses and weapons, and retreat. If he defeats me, my men will do the same."

"Are these the people who have been following us?" Marian asked.

"No," Hu said, "there are far too few men here for the amount of dust raised behind us. These men are probably that army's advance scouts."

"You said we had a part to play in this. What is it?" Trouble asked.

Hu sighed. "You are not *amah'hashi*, so for the purposes of this challenge, you are property."

Marian bristled. "Do you expect us to simply turn ourselves over to those... those... men?"

Hu met her glare with calm assurance. "I expect to win. Isih'Luku's swordsmanship looked sloppy as he delivered the *inse'le*. The challenge."

"It looked pretty damned impressive to me," Baxter said.

"You do not have my training," Hu said. "I will defeat him. Trust me."

"Mentioning trust," I said, "do you trust them to live up to their end of the... *inse'le*? If you win?"

"It is possible they will do so, but the Isifith'Ifithi are more criminals than *amah'hashi*. They are not to be trusted," Hu said. "You should be ready for a fight, should they choose the path of dishonor."

"You still have not answered my question," Marian said. "What happens if you lose?"

"My men will honor the code of the *inse'le*, lay down their weapons, and walk away. You are not *amah'hashi*, so the code doesn't bind you. But my men will not help you if you choose to fight." Hu shrugged at our displeased expressions. "It is our way."

Hu turned from us and strode towards Isih'Luku. He stopped ten feet from the other man, flourished his sword, ran through a similar series of cuts and slashes before driving his point into the ground before him. "I am Isseehu'Lu, ukateni of the Inlizyo ka Bomvu."

The two men stared at each other in the flickering light as the torch wielders formed a wide circle around the two men. The circle encompassed us, too, which none of us liked. I motioned my friend backwards, and we pushed ourselves into the gap between two of Luku's men. They frowned at us, but moved far enough apart to let us stand between them. They also drew their swords, probably as a warning to us to stay put.

Baxter stuck his head between Trouble and me, and whispered, "Please tell me you both have your blasters?"

In an equally low voice, I said, "Under my shirt, in the waistband of my pants."

"Same," Trouble whispered.

Baxter cut his eyes at Marian, who had her eyes fixed on the two swordsmen, and raised his eyebrows. I shrugged, but Trouble inclined her head slightly. Relief flooded Baxter's face, no doubt because he had no combat experience. Blasters are splendid weapons against swordsmen—*if* the swordsmen aren't standing next to you.

From the look on her face, Trouble understood our situation all too well. Her eyes met mine. She tilted her head towards the man to her right and raised her eyebrows. I nodded and tilted my head towards the man on the left. She nodded in return. If everything went to hell, at least we knew who we'd shoot first.

Luku suddenly grabbed his sword, leapt towards Hu, and delivered a vicious overhead blow towards him. The ring of steel on steel sounded as Hu took up his sword and blocked Luku's attack. And the fight was on.

Hu and Luku sprang apart. Luku dropped into a low fighting crouch, with his feet spread wide and a two-handed grip on his sword's hilt. Hu also fell into a fighting stance, but other than gently flexed knees remained upright. Hu kept his feet closer together, held his sword in his right hand, and extended his left arm for balance.

Luku leapt forward and slashed at Hu's head. Hu slid towards Luku's attack and caught the slashing blade with his own. Steel rasped, and the blades slid against each other as Hu guided Luku's attack harmlessly over his head.

Luku realized his powerful swing and miss left his chest unprotected and fell backward. Hu's riposte scraped Luku's right shoulder as he dropped. Luku turned the fall into a roll and came up onto his feet.

The combatants shuffled forward and back. Circled each other. Feinted. Withdrew. Clashed blades.

The right shoulder of Luku's shirt darkened, the first sign Hu's riposte drew blood. Hu thrust to Luku's left, and Luku easily beat Hu's blade aside. Hu advanced. Luku retreated. Hu thrust to Luku's right, and Luku beat the blade aside again. But not before Hu's sword sliced a hole through Luku's billowing shirt.

Luku circled backwards, and Hu slid easily after him. Hu repeated his thrust at Luku's right shoulder. Luku deflected the blade again, but not before Hu's sword sliced another hole in Luku's shirt.

Hu thrust to the right a third time. Cut Luku's shirt a third time. Then a fourth. And a fifth.

Within a minute, the right side of Luku's shirt was nothing but tatters. And each thrust got closer to striking Luku before Luku beat it aside. Murmurs broke out among Luku's men as their leader's sword drooped. His reactions slowed. His breath came in gasps. Sweat sprang out on Luku's face and glistened in the torchlight. And fear filled his eyes.

Luku stopped circling and scuttled towards the men ringing the duel. Hu followed, but kept to his steady, relentless pace. Hu's wary eyes flicked between Luku and the men standing behind him, ever watchful for treachery.

Before Hu reached him, Luku took a big step forward. Then he dragged his trailing foot forward, and a pile of scraped dirt gathered before Luku's foot. Luku kicked up with his trailing foot. Hu drew his sword arm in front of his eyes, protecting them from the flying dirt.

Luku leapt forward. Raised his sword high overhead. Swung down with all his might at Hu's unprotected head.

Hu's men gasped in horror, and so did we Earthers.

But Hu dodged to the right. Luku's blade passed so closely it ripped Hu's left sleeve.

Then the point of Luku's sword buried itself in the ground and stuck. Hu kicked Luku's legs out from under him. Put his sword to Luku's throat.

Hu's voice rang out. "Yield."

Then the treachery Hu watched for earlier transpired. Behind Hu, one of Luku's men drew his sword, took two quick steps forward, and raised his sword to stab Hu in the back.

Crack!

A blaster bolt seared the night air. It struck the hand holding the up-raised sword and blew the hand off the arm. The sword, with the hand still wrapped around the hilt, spun into the air.

Crack!

A second blaster bolt lanced out and struck the spinning blade.

All eyes locked on Marian and the blaster she held in a steady, two-handed grip. With almost casual self assurance, Marian said, "I fired the second shot to show the first one wasn't just a lucky shot."

Trouble and I were just as surprised as everyone else who had watched the duel. But we wrenched our attention from Marian, drew our blasters, and trained them on Luku's men who stood to either side of us.

Trouble's tone matched Marian's as she said, "I never miss at this range. Drop your sword."

No one moved for a moment. Then Luku gave a sharp yelp of pain as Hu pricked Luku's neck with his sword. "Order your men to drop their weapons, relinquish their property, and leave, or I will open your jugular vein."

Luku stared at Hu, his eyes wide with fear and shock. Hu waved the tip of his sword in front of Luku's eyes, and Luku shouted, "Do it! Do as he says."

Fifteen minutes later, Luku and his men slunk off into the desert, leaving Hu and his men richer by twenty-eight horses and as many swords.

Trouble turned to Marian. "That. Was. Incredible."

"I had no idea you could shoot like that," I added.

A smile lit her face. "I was on the Academy shooting team and placed third in the Earth collegiate championships my senior year."

"Are you hiding any other secret superpowers?" Trouble asked.

Before Marian responded, Hu bowed before her. "I thank you, Umna'Enle."

Marian's smile vanished. "I tell you, I'm not that woman."

Hu dismissed her protest with a wave. "You attacked only to defend, and did not shoot to kill. Just as I would expect from the daughter of Um'Vikeeli, the protector god."

"Just..." Marian looked at her feet. "Just drop it, okay? And call me Marian."

"As you wish, Marian," Hu said.

Since everyone was wide awake, Hu's men fixed breakfast and began breaking camp. By the time the sun peeked over the distant horizon, we were ready to move on. Marian rode by herself, silent and uncommunicative.

We spotted the Heart of Mars' vast camp in the distance just before noon. An hour later, we passed the sentries.

"Come, I will present you to Umba'Zo," Hu said.

"Are you sure he'll see us on such short notice?" Harmon asked.

Hu's eye cut to Marian, who looked away. He said, "I am certain."

Fifteen minutes later, we dismounted before a huge, multihued tent. Hu entered the tent alone, but almost immediately returned. "Umba'Zo will see you now."

Hu bowed to Marian and offered his arm. She blushed, but took it, and we followed them into the tent.

A powerfully built man waited for us. But he only had eyes for Marian. He approached her, went down on one knee, and gently took her hands. "Umna'Enle. At long last, you have returned."

Marian stared at him, shock and surprise written on her face. Her mouth opened and closed three times. Then, in a hoarse whisper, she said, "Inli'Ziyo?"

Joy lit Inli'Ziyo's face. "I feared you would not recognize me, beloved!"

Shock and uncertainty filled Marian's face. "Wha—?"

But the man kneeling before her was too caught up in his moment of rapture to notice. "I have spent lifetimes searching for you, Umna'Enle." He held his red arm next to Marian's pale one. "But I could have torn Mars apart and never have found you. For you were on another world."

Hu leaned close to Trouble and me, and whispered, "I told you it was not my tale to tell."

Inli'Ziyo came to his feet. The top of Marian's head barely reached his shoulders. Inli'Ziyo brushed his fingers through Marian's hair. "The color suits you, my one, my only love. And you..." He put two fingers under Marian's chin, raised her head, and gazed into her eyes. "You are more beautiful than I remembered."

In unison, Trouble and I murmured, "Uh oh."

Marian blinked, as if she was emerging from a trance, and looked at her feet. When she raised her head again, she wore her usual composed, controlled, and closed expression. "I'm sorry, sir, but you've confused me with someone else."

Inli'Ziyo's eyebrows arched in obvious surprise. "How can you say that when you also recognized me?"

"I... don't know," Marian said. "Maybe this strange world, aided by its thin atmosphere, is playing tricks on my mind. But..."

Marian turned and ran for the tent's exit. It took Inli'Ziyo a few seconds to recover from his surprise. Then he started after her. Only to be brought up short by Trouble's hand on his chest.

"Don't chase her. You'll only drive her farther away," Trouble said.

"Who dares—?" Inli'Ziyo's outrage died when he looked at Trouble. "I should have known you wouldn't be far from Umna'Enle's side." His lips quirked up in an amused smile. "Hello, Inka'Tazo."

Harmon leaned forward, his eyes alight with academic fervor. "I never saw that name mentioned in any of the old tales. Who is Inka'Tazo?"

"Um," Trouble said, "I think *I* am."

Harmon sighed. "I deduced as much from the situation, my dear. But how does this Inka'Tazo... I beg your pardon, Miss Tate. How do *you* fit into the story of Umna'Enle and Inli'Ziyo?"

"I... don't know," Trouble said. "I think I *should* know, though."

"It will all come back to you in time." Inli'Ziyo's gaze shifted toward Marian's flight path. "As it will for Umna'Enle."

"That's all well and good for *her*," Harmon said. "But it doesn't help *me* one bit."

"Sir," Baxter murmured, "perhaps you should wait for a better time to pursue this?"

Inli'Ziyo waved off Baxter's comment. "No, I do not object to the question." Inli'Ziyo's gaze shifted to Trouble. "Long ago, before men walked the Earth, I called Inka'Tazo the beautiful protector to my beautiful protector." He glanced back at Harmon. "Were you aware that Umna'Enle means beautiful protector in the ancient tongue?"

Harmon pulled a small notebook from his pocket and began scribbling in it. "Yes, yes. Of course." Without looking up from his writing, Harmon asked, "So Miss Tate... I mean Inka'Tazo was Umna'Enle's... what? Servant? Lady in waiting? Friend? Confidant?"

"All of that, and more." Inli'Ziyo gave an amused grunt. "On our wedding night, Inka'Tazo would not leave me alone with Umna'Enle until I convinced her I would be gentle with Umna'Enle. She did that, even though Umna'Enle had many lovers before me."

"Lovers, but none beloved." Trouble glanced at me and smiled. "That matters to a woman." She turned from Inli'Ziyo. "And on that subject, I'd better go check on Marian."

After Trouble slipped from the tent, the man Hu called Umba'Zo and Marian called Inli'Ziyo turned to me. "From the way Inka'Tazo looked at you, may I assume you have tamed and claimed her heart?"

"She has given her heart to me." I raised both hands and spread my fingers in the traditional Martian greeting. "I'm Travis Barrett, and I'd never be foolish enough to say I tamed or claimed Trouble."

Inli'Ziyo returned my greeting. "Why would you wish to claim trouble?"

"Her actual name is Tina Tate, but her younger brother nicknamed her Trouble. She prefers the nickname to her given name."

Inli'Ziyo laughed. "Do you know what Inka'Tazo means in the ancient tongue?" I shook my head, and he said, "It means troublesome friend."

I joined him in laughter. "She is most definitely troublesome. Delightfully so."

Inli'Ziyo's expression grew serious. "Grateful though I am that Mars guided Umna'Enle to me, her reaction to me suggests I was not the reason she journeyed to our world. Tell me what brings you, and what I may do to help."

I told him of my history with the pirate ship *Bloodsword*, and Space Patrol's intelligence that the pirates had a base in the Valles Marineris. Then Harmon told of his research and his conclusion that Umna'Enle's tomb lay hidden within the vast canyon.

Inli'Ziyo's eyes gleamed when Harmon finished speaking, though it was the gleam of hope rather than greed. "If we can find

Insimbi'Vik, the sword could unite the people of Mars behind our cause. We could end this foolish standoff with you Earthers, welcome you all as the brothers you are, and forge a glorious future for both our planets."

"Does that mean you'll help us find the tomb?" Harmon asked.

"And the pirate base?" I added.

"Yes, and yes," Inli'Ziyo said.

Harmon clapped his hands in obvious satisfaction. "We're going to find Insimbi'Vik, foil a gang of murderous pirates, *and* help unite the humans of two worlds!" He prodded Baxter with an elbow. "McIntosh will spend the rest of his life under the shadow I will cast over the archaeological world, eh, Baxter?"

"Quite right, sir," Baxter said.

"When do we begin?" I asked.

"As soon as we have planned the search and gathered supplies," Inli'Ziyo said.

Harmon opened his map case. "Then let's start planning!"

"Summon the other officers," Inli'Ziyo said to Hu.

Five minutes later, Inli'Ziyo explained our plan to two dozen officers, and we got busy organizing the search. Thirty minutes after we began, Trouble led Marian back into the tent. Inli'Ziyo looked up, caught Trouble's slight shake of the head, and settled for smiling at Marian. Then he turned to Trouble and asked, "Do you remember where Umna'Enle's tomb is?"

Marian shivered at the question, but Trouble gave it careful thought. "Ancient memories are coming back to me, but the geography has changed so much since we laid her to rest."

"That is true," Inli'Ziyo said, "but do any of these sites *feel* right to you?"

Without hesitation, Trouble's hand shot out and tapped the one marked Site 21. "This one. I don't know *why*, but..."

Inli'Ziyo nodded. "I have the same feeling." He looked at Hu. "You will lead the team that explores the site, and I'll accompany you."

"We'll come with you," I said.

Inli'Ziyo pointed to a senior officer and said, "Finish assigning teams to the other sites while Hu and I prepare for our departure."

Two hours later, we five Earthers and eighty-three Martians rode off in search of the tomb, the sword, and the pirates.

trouble with smugglers

FOR THE FIRST hour of our ride, Inli'Ziyo and Hu debated the best route to take to the possible tomb location, marked Site 21 on Harmon's map, assigned and dispatched outriders, and dealt with a dozen smaller details they hadn't had time to address before our hasty departure. I waited until they finished their discussion, and then Trouble and I rode up to Inli'Ziyo's side. He invited conversation with an open smile.

Trouble immediately asked, "What are we supposed to call you?"

Inli'Ziyo's eyebrows arched in apparent surprise. "Of all people, Inka'Tazo, why do you need to ask this question?"

"I *was* Inka'Tazo. I *am* Tina Tate."

Inli'Ziyo nodded. "I believe I understand. You wish me to use your current name."

"I only have vague memories of my life as Inka'Tazo. Answering to it feels... odd," Trouble said. "Also, only people who don't know me well call me Tina, or Miss Tate. My friends call me Trouble."

"Am I to be counted among your friends?" Inli'Ziyo asked.

She flashed her gigawatt smile. "We've known each other since the literal dawn of time. If that doesn't make us friends, I don't know what does."

"Very well, Trouble. As for me..." He shrugged. "I discovered I was Inli'Ziyo reborn more than half a lifetime ago. I give the name Umba'Zo among those unready for my true identity. But I am Inli'Ziyo to my men." He flashed a bright smile of his own. "And to those I call friend."

I looked at Marian, who somehow isolated herself while riding with over eighty people. "Marian is... Let's say she's stubborn. Don't you think calling yourself Inli'Ziyo will end up pushing her away from you?"

Inli'Ziyo followed my gaze, and his lingered on Marian. At last, he said, "Umna'Enle always was strong willed. With so many men vying for her favor—and for her sword—she had to be. Though her mind resists, her heart knows our true identities. Calling me by the name given to me at my most recent birth will not help her mind to accept the truth."

"But you'll still call *her* Marian?" Trouble asked. "She only learned she was Umna'Enle a few days ago. If her visions of that life are like mine, they're more like dreams than true memories. If you push her too hard to be the Umna'Enle you remember, you'll just drive her farther from you."

Inli'Ziyo gave a slow nod. "You always were insightful, Inka... I mean, Trouble. I have waited for lifetimes uncounted for Umna'Enle's return. If I must wait a few days longer, I shall."

Hu rode up with more questions for Inli'Ziyo, so we backed off and let them get on with the business of managing the expedition. After a moment, Trouble looked at me. "What?"

"Hm? What what?"

"You want to ask me a question, but you're holding back." I cocked an eyebrow at her. Trouble moved her horse closer to me, took my hand, and smiled gently. "I'm insightful, remember?"

"I'm just wondering how you're taking all of this," I waved at Marian, Inli'Ziyo, and at her, "without freaking out. I mean, it's one thing to talk about you being a Traveller when it was just a weird Martian belief. But to suddenly discover your soul really traveled from Mars to Earth? To discover you have lived thousands of lifetimes? Why doesn't that overwhelm you, as it does Marian?"

Trouble silently considered my question. She took a long time, but finally said, "I think it's because I'm happier as Trouble than I was as Inka'Tazo."

"You are?" Trouble nodded, and I asked, "Why?"

Trouble released my hand, caught me behind the neck, pulled our faces together, and kissed me so thoroughly the men of the Heart of Mars began hooting around us. When she ended the kiss, Trouble looked at me, cocked her head, and raised her eyebrows in silent inquiry.

"Eloquently put," I said. "You should explain that to me often."

Trouble looked willing to lean into me and offer another explanation, but my comm buzzed. I pulled the comm from my pocket, accepted the call, and said, "It's about time you checked in, Rita."

"Hello to you, too, Boss." Reproach sounded in Rita's voice. "It's good to hear your voice."

"If all you wanted to do was hear my voice, you could have called earlier," I said. "Like I *expected* you to do."

"Were you worried about me?" Rita asked.

"Of course." I knew she was fishing for that answer, and I didn't mind giving it to her. Besides, it was the truth. "I'm worried about Dave, too. Is he okay?"

"Sure, Boss. Hayslett's been up and working hard since a few hours after you left."

"Have those four legionnaires been that busy?"

"Them? Not a chance, Boss. They just lounged next to the gate and drank. Or went into town and drank."

"Then what has Dave been working on?"

"Ban told us the four drunks were rotating off gate guard duty today. So Dave got Ban to requisition a couple of recon hover bikes, and Dave's been tinkering with them ever since. Something about redirecting the exhaust. I got no idea why. But there's no way I'm going to show ignorance to Hayslett and ask him."

"Don't worry, Rita. I know why he's doing it." Rita was silent long enough that I asked, "You still there, Rita?"

"Yeah, Boss."

"Then why didn't you say something?"

"Because I was waiting for *you* to explain why Dave is fiddling with the hover bikes' exhaust."

"Oh, sorry, Rita. Dave's trying to cut down on the dust the bikes blow into the air. If the four drunk guards go somewhere besides the town, he and Ban can follow them without raising a telltale cloud of dust."

"Huh. That's... kind of clever," Rita admitted. She added, "Don't you dare tell Hayslett I said that, Boss!"

"My lips are sealed," I said. "Is that all?"

"No, Boss. I just needed to tell you that stuff before I told you why I called." Rita paused again. I knew from long experience she did it for dramatic effect. After five seconds, she said, "The four drunks got four riding horses and a dozen pack mules from the stables. They just rode out of the fort and went away from town."

"Towards the canyon?"

"You got it, Boss."

"I assume Dave and Ban are following?"

"We're giving them a thirty-minute head start, then heading after them."

"We? You can't ride a hover bike."

"No, but Hayslett is going to pull me along behind his bike. I hover just as high as it does."

"I don't know, Rita. That sounds dangerous."

"Not as dangerous as sticking around this fort, Boss. Ban says the scum here would strip me for spare parts an hour after he and Hayslett left. Ain't no way I'm waiting around for that!"

"No, you're right, Rita. Just tell Dave to be careful with you. Trouble and I don't want to have to get a new Robosec."

"You got it, Boss. Hayslett is walking this way with rope, so it looks like we're about ready to go. I'll call again when I have something to report."

"Okay, Rita. Bye."

I disconnected and relayed the conversation to Trouble. She considered the news, then said, "It sounds like the four weapons smugglers are going to get more weapons to smuggle."

"That's what it sounds like to me, too."

"Do you think Dave, Rita, and Ban will end up where we're headed?"

"I hope so." The thought of the trio stumbling across the *Bloodsword's* base by themselves sent a shiver down my spine. "I truly hope so."

The sun hung low on the Martian horizon before we stopped for the night. Hu politely refused my offer to help set up camp, and I soon learned why. Without orders from Hu, his men established the camp with practiced efficiency. By the time darkness settled over us, a dozen crackling fires ringed the inner camp and Hu's men tended cooking pots hung above half the fires.

Since I had nothing else to do, I pulled out my comm and called Rita. She answered immediately, and I detected a note of displeasure in her voice when she said, "Yeah, Boss?"

"What's wrong?"

"What makes you think anything's wrong, Boss?"

"That's not an answer, Rita."

"Gosh, it sure is amazing how you figured that out, Boss. Maybe you oughta become a private eye or something."

I heard Dave speak from close by Rita. "This is going to take forever if you don't hold still."

"What's going to take forever?" I asked.

"Don't ask," Rita snapped.

"I already did."

Dave called, "If that's you, Travis, tell your damned Robosec to stop bouncing around on her hover field. It's making this job way harder than it needs to be."

"What job?" I asked. "What's going on?"

"I told you not to ask, Boss," Rita said.

"Too late. I already asked." Rita didn't answer. I heaved an irritated sigh. "Do I have to order you to tell me?"

Rita gasped. "You wouldn't do that to me, would you, Boss?"

Rita is a person to me, but she's a product for her manufacturer. Rossum's software includes automatic obedience routines for any lawful command issued by the Robosec's owner that ends with the phrase 'that is a direct order.' I respect Rita's free will and have never compelled her obedience.

"I don't want to, Rita," I said. "But you know what putting an end to *Bloodsword's* reign of terror means to me. You and Dave might be the ones who discover the pirate base, so anything that affects you two could affect the mission."

"It won't affect the mission, Boss." Rita spoiled her assurance by giggling.

"Dammit, Rita," Dave said, "*hold still*!"

"You never giggle, Rita," I said. "Never."

"I know, Boss, it's..." Rita giggled again. "It's embarrassing."

"If you won't tell him, I will," Dave said.

"Okay..." Rita giggled again, then said, "You remember when I told you about Hayslett redirecting the exhaust for the hover bikes, Boss?" Rita's tone sharpened. "Well, genius boy redirected some of it to blow backwards."

"And?" I asked.

"Where do you think *I* was, Boss?" Another giggle ruined Rita's snippy tone. "I got dust all over me and in my joints."

I sighed. "Tell Dave I said to clean you up."

"No need, Boss. Hayslett's already doing that."

"Then what's the problem?"

"It turns out..." Rita giggled again. "I'm ticklish, Boss!"

"You get polished every time you go in for service, Rita. Why didn't you already know that?"

"Rossum techs shut me down while they work on me," she giggled, "and don't start me up again until they're done."

"But you don't have nerve endings. How—?"

"I bet it's some programmer's idea of a funny joke," Rita said. "*I* know I shouldn't feel Hayslett wiping the dust off me, but my programming doesn't care."

"Almost done, Rita," Dave said. "And... Done."

"About time," Rita said. "Okay, Boss. Whatcha need?"

"We just stopped for the night, so I thought I'd check in with you. Any news?"

"I said I'd comm if anything happened, Boss," Rita said. "Did I comm?"

I sighed. "No."

"Then you oughta figure nothing happened, right, Boss?"

"But you could have run into trouble and been unable to comm. I needed to reassure myself that nothing happened to you."

"That's sweet, Boss," Rita said. "But what would you have done if I didn't answer? You can't come looking for us without putting the real mission at risk. Am I right?"

"You're right, Rita. But now I know nothing happened to you. That's one thing I don't have to worry about tonight."

"You know I'd've called later, Boss."

"I do, Rita. But now you don't have to. Unless something happens." I paused. "Um, nothing is happening right now, I guess?"

"You got it in one, Boss. The four drunk guard guys stopped for the night in a gully or something. It took Ban an hour to find a place where we could look down on them without being spotted. He's been keeping an eye on them while Hayslett cleaned me off." Rita's voice dropped to a whisper. "Me and Hayslett just got to the lookout spot." Rita sniffed with disdain. "And—gee, what a shocker—those four bums are passing a bottle around."

"It looks like you, Dave, and Ban are in for an exciting night," I said. "So I'll sign off and leave you to it."

"Okay, Boss. And don't worry. I'll comm you if anything interesting happens."

"Bye, Rita."

"Bye, Boss."

I relayed the conversation to Trouble and Marian, then we rested our aching bodies and waited for Hu's men to finish cooking dinner. I must have dozed off, because the buzzing of my comm awakened me fifteen minutes later.

I took the call. "What's up, Rita?"

"Something's happening here, Boss," Rita said in a low tone. "We got lights coming up the gully towards the camp below."

All vestiges of sleep fled. "What kind of lights?"

"Hayslett says it's a truck. Earth make, not Martian."

"The pirates?"

"Don't know yet, Boss, but the four bums down there don't look worried or anything. They're just standing there waiting."

A minute passed before Rita said, "The truck stopped just outside of the bums' camp... Two doors opening... Couple of men got out." In an excited whisper, Rita added, "They ain't Martians, Boss. Looks like an Asian and a European guy."

A voice nearby spoke, but it was too quiet for me to make out the words, or even tell whether it was Ban or Dave speaking. But Rita said, "Ban says we should be the only Earthers up here." Rita paused for a second, then said, "It looks like we found two of the pirates, Boss."

"Hang on for a minute, Rita." I waved Trouble and Marian over to me. "I'm going to put my comm on speaker so Trouble and Marian can hear you, too."

The two women settled on the ground in front of me. I switched the comm to speaker, and said, "I'm going to mute the comm on this end, Rita. I don't want noise from our camp coming through the comm on your end."

"We're seventy or eighty yards from the smugglers, so it probably won't matter, Boss. But better safe and all that."

I put the comm on the ground between the three of us, and Rita described the situation for the benefit of Trouble and Marian. "We're on a ledge looking over a camp those four drunks from the fort set up in a gully. Two Earther men just drove up in a truck, and now they're talking to the Martian guys."

Rita fell silent. I assumed she was waiting for something to happen, and said, "Ban told Rita we're the only Earthers currently approved for travel in this area."

Excitement lit Trouble's eyes. "So the guys in the truck are probably pirates?"

"I think so," I said. "Trucks need supplies and, in an environment like this, a lot more service than usual. That means it came from a base, something smugglers aren't real big on. Smugglers rely on speed and stealth, and wouldn't waste precious cargo space on a delivery truck."

"But pirates *have* to have a base to support their ship," Trouble said.

Rita broke her silence. "Looks like they're done talking, Boss. Everybody's walking around to the back of the truck... The driver opened the cargo door and... Yep, two Martians are carrying a crate around to the truck's front." A voice murmured in the background, and Rita added, "Hayslett thinks they want to examine the cargo using the truck's headlights." Her vocorder switched to a grudging tone. "I guess that makes sense."

"Okay, the truck's driver just got between the Martians and the crate... Oh, he's entering a passcode on the box's lock and he doesn't want the Martians seeing the code. Too bad for him, 'cause we can see the keypad from up here... Hayslett's watching with his binoculars, and he says the code is... 10171981... Don't know what we'll do with the code but I got it... Anyway, the driver moved out of the way so the Martian drunks can get to the crate."

"One of them is opening the crate... The Martians look excited." Rita paused for ten seconds. We heard two muffled curses come from near Rita, then she said, "Uh oh. The pirates brought blaster rifles this time."

I glanced at Marian, whose lips compressed into a thin, angry line, and Trouble, who returned my look, and asked, "Is this the first time the pirates smuggled rifles?"

I shrugged, but held any comment when a voice murmured near Rita. She said, "Uh, Boss, can you take the comm off mute? Ban wants to talk to you."

I debated turning off speaker mode on my comm, but the camp was quiet enough that I decided not to. I unmuted the comm. "Okay, we're unmuted. I left it on speaker so Marian and Trouble can hear what Ban has to say."

Rita relayed my words to Ban, and random clicks and pops sounded from my comm as Rita handed her comm to Ban. Then he asked, "Can you hear me, Travis?"

"Yes, you're loud and clear."

"Rita told you of the blaster rifles?"

"Yes."

"The four soldiers from the fort are busy unloading crates now. Do you know how many blaster rifles fit in a standard shipping crate?"

"Six to ten, depending on the make and model. The crate usually has an assortment of tools, spare parts, and extra energy cells, too."

"I thought as much. Let us see how many crates those Earthers brought with them." Ten minutes passed, then said, "There are twenty-four crates, Travis."

"Rita told me the soldiers brought a dozen pack mules. Two crates per mule. Mules can handle that load easily."

"How do you know this, Travis?" Ban asked.

"I grew up on a farm."

"Ah. Well, you are correct. The soldiers are loading the mules, and the mules appear unbothered by the load."

That surprised me. "Do you think the four soldiers will risk traveling in the dark?"

"From the liquor bottles sticking out of their packs, I doubt it."

"Then why pack the mules now? That's not good for the animals."

"I doubt these men care. And they will almost certainly have hangovers in the morning." Ban paused for a moment, then said, "But this is a good development."

"What makes you say that?"

"If my plan works, it will save me a lot of time."

"What plan? What are you talking about, Ban?"

Instead of answering, Ban asked, "How many men travel with you?"

"Eighty-something. I don't know the exact number."

"You will need more men than that to attack the pirate base, Travis."

That was a concern of mine, too. "It's not an ideal situation, but it's better than the half-a-dozen people I originally planned for. And it's not like I can whistle up more men at a moment's notice."

"That is true, but..." Ban paused for a second, then said, "What if those eighty-something men were more heavily armed? Say, with blaster rifles supplied by the pirates, themselves?"

"You want to steal the rifles from the guards?"

"Yes. They will almost certainly drink themselves into a stupor. Even if they don't, I can handle four drunks."

"But you're supposed to follow the pirates, Ban. They'll almost certainly lead you straight back to their base."

"We have two recon hover bikes, Travis. Dave and Rita will follow the truck. I'll stay here, wait for the men to get drunk, and then steal the blaster rifles."

I searched for flaws in Ban's plan. Assuming the four soldiers got drunk—and that seemed like a safe assumption—it sounded as close to foolproof as a plan could be. I looked at Marian and Trouble, and raised my eyebrows. They both nodded.

"Okay, Ban. Steal the blaster rifles."

trouble with expectations

BAN RETURNED the comm to Rita for the wrap up. The four guards from the fort paid the two Earther men, the Earthers returned to their truck, and they drove away. We agreed Ban would communicate with us through her. She signed off so she and Dave could follow the pirates' truck.

"Now what?" Trouble asked.

I pocketed my comm. "We eat, and then get some sleep."

"I don't know if I even *can* sleep," Marian said.

"I know how you feel, but you need to try," I said. "Tired people make mistakes, and I doubt we can afford many of those when we face the pirates."

I saw Hu heading our way and stood to greet him, as did Trouble and Marian. Hu greeted us with a nod and said, "Inli'Ziyo requests you three join him for the evening meal."

I ignored the imploring look Marian turned my way. "We'd be delighted."

Hu turned, motioned for us to follow, and headed toward the center of camp and Inli'Ziyo. Marian turned away, obviously planning on staying put. I caught her arm and pulled her along with me.

"Release me, Mr. Barrett," she demanded.

"No."

"I don't want to eat with that man."

"Space Patrol officers have to do a lot of things they don't want to do."

"Give me one good reason I should do this."

I waved vaguely at the surrounding camp. "God willing, these men will put their lives on the line for our mission. The least you can do is honor them by dining with their leader."

In a small voice, Marian said, "Oh."

"Did you think I was trying to push you into Inli'Ziyo's arms?" I asked.

Marian shrugged. "Or his bed."

"You and Inli'Ziyo are adults. I think you're more than capable of figuring out your relationship on your own. But..." I stared hard into Marian's eyes. "You need to decide what's more important to you right now. Your relationship with Inli'Ziyo or your mission to put an end to the *Bloodsword's* reign?"

Marian's shields went up, her lips compressed to a line, and she glared at me. "I shouldn't have to dignify that question with an answer."

I met her glare with one of my own. "I agree. But your behavior since we met Inli'Ziyo says otherwise."

"The *Bloodsword*," she spat. "Satisfied?" Without waiting for an answer, Marian pulled free of my grip and went to walk next to Hu.

Trouble took my hand. "Did you have to be so hard on her?"

"Yes. She spent all afternoon staring at Inli'Ziyo, sometimes with longing, and sometimes in fear. She needs to remember the dangers ahead of us have nothing to do with Inli'Ziyo's romance of Umna'Enle, and everything to do with the most dangerous pirates in the solar system. I shocked her into doing that. If it means she ends up loathing me, I don't care." I stared at Marian as she held herself ramrod straight while walking next to Hu. "Besides, I can't rid myself of the notion that the success or failure of this mission hinges on Marian."

"I have the same feeling," Trouble said.

Inli'Ziyo stood at our approach, and Marian's already-rigid posture stiffened even more. But she didn't turn away from him, nor did her expression alter.

"Welcome, my Earther friends." Inli'Ziyo motioned to the fire burning before his tent. "Please join me."

Marian immediately sat on the opposite side of the fire from our host, and Trouble and I each took seats flanking Marian. If Marian's reaction dismayed Inli'Ziyo, he didn't show it. He sat where he'd been before and turned my way.

"I saw you speaking on your communications device a few minutes ago," he said. "Hu told me of your companions and their mission. Have they had any success?"

"They have," I replied, and quickly outlined the news Rita shared with me.

Inli'Ziyo listened attentively, then asked, "The soldier, Bangaz'Ri, is from *Kaba Udoti*. Did he tell you what the fort's name means?"

"Yes," Marian said. "Fort Garbage."

"And did he tell you why it has that name?"

"It's where the Legion discards its worst legionnaires," Marian snapped. "What of it?"

"Yet you put your trust in this man, who was himself banished to the garbage heap?"

"Captain Ri sacrificed a promising career in the hopes of discovering the source of the Earth weapons smuggled to the warlords, gangs, and tribes waging war on his home country of Kah'Freon."

"He sounds like an honorable man. I look forward to meeting him." Inli'Ziyo looked at me. "I have taken no interest in Earther weapons in the past, preferring the weapons of Mars. But we face steep odds against these pirates of yours. Should your legionnaire friend successfully steal the blaster rifles, can you teach my men how to use them?"

"Absolutely," I said. "As can Trouble, Marian, and our friend Dave."

"That is good." Inli'Ziyo stared into the fire for a moment. "If fortune smiles on us, we won't need your planet's weapons for long."

"Why is that?" Marian asked.

Inli'Ziyo smiled at her. "Because your sword also lies within the tomb. Only you may draw Insimbi'Vik. Only you can choose the sword's bearer. And only Insimbi'Vik's bearer can lead us to victory."

Marian stared across the fire at Inli'Ziyo. "Do you honestly expect us to believe in a magic sword?"

"Neither belief nor disbelief changes what *is*." Inli'Ziyo caught Marian's gaze and smiled. "You will understand when you hold Insimbi'Vik again."

Marian held his gentle gaze, and her defenses slowly unraveled before our eyes. Her lips turned up in a tentative smile, then she leaned back and stared up into the infinite sky above us. She sighed. "What a beautiful sight. There are few places on Earth where you can see the stars so clearly."

"Surely you can see them with more clarity from space?" Inli'Ziyo asked.

"The stars are too clear in space. They're... I don't quite know how to explain it. Stark. Untwinkling. Uncaring." Marian pulled her knees up to her chin, wrapped her arms around her legs, and looked like the twenty-three-year-old woman she was. She lowered her head and gazed at Inli'Ziyo with a wistful expression. "I envy your certainty about your life." She gave a rueful laugh. "Or should I say *lives*?"

I held my breath, afraid Inli'Ziyo would press Marian to accept herself as Umna'Enle. But I guess a man learns *something* about women after thousands of lifetimes. Inli'Ziyo simply smiled and said, "Certainty is a comfort. I believe your companions, Travis and Trouble, will agree."

I looked across the fire and into Trouble's blue eyes. She met my gaze, smiled, and said, "Definitely."

Then the camp cook bustled up with bowls of steaming stew

and mugs of water, ending our moment of shared contentment. To my surprise, Marian didn't raise her shields after her moment of vulnerability. She joined in light conversation as we ate and even told a joke. She didn't tell it well, but the simple fact that she tried amazed me. I rewarded her attempt with a laugh, as did Trouble and Inli'Ziyo.

After we finished eating, Inli'Ziyo had Hu bring out a bottle of Martian liquor. He splashed some into our cups, raised his cup, and said, "To vengeance for you, my friends, and unity for my people."

"I'll drink to that," I said, and drained my cup. The liquor tasted unusual, as befitted its Martian origin, but I felt the familiar warmth of alcohol in my stomach. I nodded to Inli'Ziyo. "Thank you for dinner. It's been a long day, and tomorrow might be even longer. If you'll excuse us, we'll return to our fire and get some sleep."

"May the gods watch over you," Inli'Ziyo said. "But should their attention be elsewhere, know that my men will also keep watch."

Marian walked next to Trouble and me as we picked our way through the camp. Harmon and Baxter approached the fire from another direction. Both wore satisfied smiles, which led me to believe they'd eaten with some of Inli'Ziyo's men, and plied the men with academic questions about life among the *amah'hashi*.

Just before we reached our fire, Marian said, "Thank you."

I looked at her in surprise. "For what?"

"For making me go with you. For giving me the verbal kick in the backside I needed."

"Don't worry about it."

"That's easier said than done." Marian caught my arm, stopped walking, and looked back and forth between Trouble and me. "I don't mean to be so difficult." She shrugged. "I'm just... Just..."

"Just bearing the full weight and expectations of Space Patrol on a pair of twenty-three-year-old shoulders?"

Marian's eyes widened at my words. "That's not how I'd put it."

"But it's true, isn't it?" I asked.

"And," Trouble said, "that was before we learned Travellers aren't just some weird Martian myth."

Marian nodded, and then she asked, "Miss Tate... Trouble... Could we talk for a minute?" She glanced at me. "Privately?"

I didn't even wait for Trouble's assenting nod. "I'll just return to the fire and tell Harmon and Baxter what we've learned since we made camp."

It only took two minutes to bring the archaeologists up to speed, but Marian and Trouble talked quietly for thirty minutes. When they joined us around the fire, Marian went straight to her sleeping pallet. I raised my eyebrows at Trouble and got a shake of her head in return. I gave her a quick kiss, and then we crawled under our blankets. The last thing I saw before I fell asleep was Marian, lost in thought and staring at the twinkling stars.

▭

PHYSICAL AND MENTAL exhaustion carried me into a sleep filled with nightmares I hadn't suffered through since I met Trouble. Of the *Bloodsword* hammering my old ship, the *Soteria*. Of grotesque pirates dancing wildly around the dead from my crew. Of a chorus of fifty copies of Commodore Jacobson, the commander whose cowardice left my crew and ship facing the vastly more powerful *Bloodsword* alone, singing a dirge with savage glee.

A buzz cut through the singing in my dream. Neither the capering pirates nor the Jacobson chorus reacted to the sound. In my dream, I turned my head right and left, searching for the source of the buzz. I couldn't find one and did my best to ignore the insistent sound. But it kept calling to me.

Calling?

Me?

My comm!

I opened my eyes and fumbled for the comm I kept next to my sleeping pallet. My hand found the comm at the same time I heard the soft rustle of clothes against a blanket as Trouble rolled my way. I sat up, accepted the call, and brought the comm to my ear. "Is that you, Rita?"

"Who else, Boss?"

"What's happening?"

"Nothing, but in a weird way." Before I could ask what she meant by that, Rita continued. "The pirate truck Dave and me followed? It took a winding path to the side of the canyon. Then it stopped in front of a sheer wall that goes straight up for about four hundred yards."

"What did it do then?"

"That's the weird part, Boss. It's just sitting there, facing the wall."

"Did either of the pirates get out of the truck?"

"Nope."

"Huh." My mind raced as I sought an explanation for the pirates' behavior. I found one almost immediately. "Maybe you're near the pirate base, and someone is scanning the truck to make sure they're alone? Are you and Dave hidden well enough to avoid detection, if I'm right?"

"Relax, Boss. Hayslett is just as paranoid as you. He hid us and the hover bike behind a boulder, and is using a Martian version of a fiber-optic periscope to watch what the pirates are doing."

"You're sure no one can see you two?"

"We can't even see the top of that big cliff from here, Boss. Hayslett says unless one of the pirates has x-ray vision or some-thing like that, we should be safe."

"What do *you* say about your position, Rita?"

In a reluctant tone, Rita said, "Hayslett's right."

Dave said something in the background, and Rita snapped, "No, I'm not going to say that a second time. You'll just have to replay it in your memory." Dave murmured another comment. Rita replied, "It's not my fault you humans have faulty memories. You'll just have to live with it, Hayslett, 'cause I can't imagine I'll ever say those two words together again."

"Stop bickering with Dave and—"

"Hang on, Boss. Hayslett says something is happening." Dave spoke again, and Rita said, "Hayslett wants me to hold the comm to his ear so he can tell you what he's seeing."

A second later, Dave asked, "Can you hear me, Travis?"

"Yes. What's happening?"

"Half of that big cliff face just flickered and disappeared. It looked like solid rock one second, the next it was a huge opening in the cliff."

"Can you see inside?"

"Oh, yeah. Clear as day, because it's got artificial lighting inside. It's got to be one of those tombs Harmon went on about. There's a cavernous chamber in there."

"And?"

"Jack. Pot."

"Do you think it's the pirate base?"

"Definitely." Dave was silent for a second, then said, "The *Bloodsword* is docked inside, big as life and twice as ugly."

"You're sure?"

"I was with you on the *Soteria*, Travis. Do you think I'll *ever* forget what that ship looks like?"

"No, of course not. It's just..." My voice trailed off. "It's just..."

In a gentle tone, Dave said, "You never believed you'd get a chance to avenge the *Soteria's* crew?"

"Yeah."

"I hate to be the bearer of bad news, but if you don't get a move on, you might not get a chance today, either."

"What's going on?"

"Assuming the pirates use the same packing crates everyone

else in the solar system uses, they're busy loading supplies onto the *Bloodsword* as we speak."

A sinking sensation formed in the pit of my stomach. "Can you tell how close they are to finishing?"

"It looks like they still have a lot of stuff to load. They probably won't finish until after sunrise."

"That gives us some more time. I can't imagine they'd take off in broad daylight. What do—"

"Crap."

"What? Is the ship moving?"

"It wasn't, and I'd bet the *Lightning's Hand* that it still isn't. But the holographic image hiding the entrance just reappeared. Oh, and the truck is gone. It probably drove inside while I was looking at the *Bloodsword*."

"Good work, Dave. Give me your coordinates, so we can come meet you."

Dave rattled off the coordinates. I didn't even have to check Harmon's map to know he and Rita were at site 21. The same site where Trouble and Inli'Ziyo thought Umna'Enle's tomb was hidden.

"Got it," I said. "You and Rita stay out of sight until we get there."

"When will that be?" Dave asked.

"As soon as possible. We're about nine miles from you as the crow flies. No guess how far that is as the horse trots, but figure on two to three hours. I don't suppose Ban has arrived with the blaster rifles?"

"No. He's got farther to go, and he can't push the horses or the mules too hard. Last time Rita talked to him, Ban figured he'd get here sometime shortly after noon."

"Okay. I'm going to go talk to Hu and Inli'Ziyo. We'll leave as soon as they deem it safe for the horses."

"Sounds good." Dave paused for a minute, then added, "I won't let you down this time, Travis."

"You didn't let me down last time, Dave."

"You know what I mean."

"Yeah, I do."

"I've been dreaming about this day for six years, Travis. Let's make damned sure those bastards pay for what they did to our crew mates and ship."

"That's the plan, Dave." I ended the comm call and turned to Trouble, who was just visible in the early morning light. "Wake everyone up. We're going pirate hunting."

trouble with stealth

AS TROUBLE GAVE Marian a gentle shake, I rose and picked my way through the sleeping *amah'hashi* to Inli'Ziyo's fire. He must have been awake, because he sat up when I approached him.

"You have news?" Inli'Ziyo asked.

I nodded. "The pirates our friends followed led them straight to the pirate base."

"Is it also the tomb of Umna'Enle?"

"From Dave's description, I'm pretty sure it's *a* tomb. And it's at the same coordinates as site 21, the one you and Trouble both feel is the right location for Umna'Enle's tomb."

"But we won't know until we can search it for ourselves." Inli'Ziyo rose from his sleeping pallet and called, "Hu? Gather the patrol leaders and bring them to me."

"At once." Hu hopped to his feet and walked towards the nearest fire.

Inli'Ziyo turned back to me. "Gather your four companions and return. We have much to discuss before we leave."

Five minutes later, Harmon, Baxter, Marian, Trouble, Hu, ten other *amah'hashi*, and I gathered around Inli'Ziyo. The reborn Martian warrior gathered us with his intense gaze and said, "The time we have long awaited is close at hand. A friend of our two Travellers has found the pirate base we spoke of yesterday. Dr. Harmon selected its location as one of several final resting places for Umna'Enle." The Martians among us glanced at Marian, who did her best to ignore the attention. Inli'Ziyo's next words drew their attention back to him. "Trouble, she who was Inka'Tazo in a past life, and I both feel it is the tomb. Which means it's also the final resting place for Insimbi'Vik."

Hu and the ten patrol leaders nodded and murmured in agreement with the conclusion. To my surprise, Inli'Ziyo looked at me. "Travis, would you give us your best guess how many pirates reside within the base?"

"Considering the size of the *Bloodsword*, we should expect at least thirteen hundred. Fifteen hundred is more likely. That includes the ship's crew and support personnel."

Hu and the patrol leaders nodded, apparently unfazed at the idea of being outnumbered fifteen or more to one. Inli'Ziyo smiled at their confidence. "We believe one *amah'hashi* is worth ten normal men, but even that equation is against us. Fortunately, another of the Travellers' friends has stolen over one hundred Earther blaster rifles and, even now, is on his way to join those who discovered the base."

"When will he arrive?" Hu asked.

Inli'Ziyo looked at me, and I said, "Our best guess is noon."

Hu thought for a moment and then turned to Inli'Ziyo. "It will only take us two hours to ride to the site marked on the map. We must assume the pirates will keep watch outside of their base. I see no way a group this large can arrive unseen by the pirates."

"You are right," Inli'Ziyo said. "That is why we will split up in patrols. *Amah'hashi* patrols pass through that area all the time, so their presence shouldn't concern the pirates on watch. As a further precaution, each patrol, but the one I lead, will follow a winding path to the base. We will appear and disappear with the terrain, hiding our numbers and confusing our enemies."

"What of your patrol?" Hu asked.

"I will take our Earther friends directly to the base. The Traveller Marian will contact a spy among the pirates, and perhaps we will find a way to safely scout the base from inside."

"Then I will ride at your side," Hu said.

"I expected nothing less, my friend," Inli'Ziyo said. "Assign routes to your patrol leaders. We leave when the sun climbs above the horizon."

Inli'Ziyo, Hu, and we five Earthers rode out forty minutes later. Hu's two-hour travel estimate proved accurate, but it took another twenty minutes and three comm calls to find Dave and Rita. I explained why there were so few of us while my companions took turns examining the cliff face through Dave's fiber optic periscope.

Hu's and Inli'Ziyo's eyes shone with excitement after they looked through the periscope. Marian wore an apprehensive expression when she relinquished the device to Trouble. And who could blame her? I sure wouldn't relish the idea of infiltrating my own tomb. But Trouble's finger tapped her lips after her turn with the periscope.

"What's wrong, Trouble?" I asked. "Do you think it's not Umna'Enle's tomb?"

She shook her head. "I'm positive it's the tomb. But that's not all." She glanced at Inli'Ziyo. "Do you remember including a hidden entrance when you designed the tomb?"

"Yes," he said. "It let us visit her final resting place even after we sealed the tomb. I looked for it when I looked through the device, but couldn't find it."

"I looked, too, and I think I found it," Trouble said. "Who wants to join me on a scouting trip inside the base?"

Most of our party jumped at Trouble's suggestion. They kept their voices low, since we were a quarter of a mile from the pirate base, but showed their excitement at the prospect of sneaking into the base.

Marian waved her arms for quiet and said, "Before we try sneaking into the pirate base, how about we follow the original Space Patrol plan?"

"What is their plan?" Hu asked.

"We've told you I'm an active duty Space Patrol officer, my primary mission was finding the pirate base, and—"

"Which you've done, lass," Harmon said.

"*And,*" Marian continued, "I'm supposed to call on a Space Patrol squadron stationed near Mars to handle the actual attack on the base."

"You told us of your search, but didn't mention the Space Patrol squadron. Why?" Inli'Ziyo asked.

Marian cast her eyes down, away from Inli'Ziyo's gaze. "I feared you wouldn't help us if you knew our plan involved an attack on Martian soil by an Earth force."

Inli'Ziyo's lips spread in a sad smile. "With every distrustful decision, you show your true self. Do you truly believe I could deny you anything, Umna'Enle?"

"Please," Marian whispered, "don't call me by that name."

Inli'Ziyo nodded. "I will wait until you are ready to acknowledge your true self." He turned to me. "But that doesn't explain why you did not tell me of this squadron."

I met his gaze and said, "The last time I trusted Space Patrol, I lost half my crew and my ship. I will never make the mistake of counting on Space Patrol again. That's why I never mentioned the squadron. That's why I agreed to Ban's plan to steal the blaster rifles. That's why I'm ready to sneak into the pirate base now." I glanced at Marian. "But nothing would make me happier than being proven wrong about Space Patrol's reliability."

"Fine," Marian said. "Let me assemble the transmitter, and I'll call the squadron."

Two minutes later, Marian turned on the transmitter, entered coordinates for the tight beam signal, activated the microphone, and said, "Traveller calling Angel. Come in Angel."

She looked at me. "The signal will take a few seconds to reach the squadron. A reply could take up to a minute, because they'll need to calculate coordinates for their tight beam reply."

"What is this tight beam?" Hu asked.

"It's a focused radio signal that's all but impossible to intercept," I said. "If she used a standard broadcast, the pirates could overhear it. From the signal's strength, they'd know it came from nearby, too. Even if they didn't send out search teams, the radio signal would put them on their guard."

Twenty seconds later, the radio crackled, and a woman's voice said, "Traveller, this is Angel." The voice paused for a second. "We, um, weren't expecting to hear from you."

Marian's posture stiffened. "Why not, Angel?"

"Command received a credible report of a *Bloodsword* attack in the asteroid belt. They sent Angel to investigate."

Marian bowed her head. "It's a trick, Angel. The *Bloodsword* is in its base, a quarter of a mile from my location."

Uncertainty entered Angel's voice. "That can't be right. The report came from the agent inside the base."

Marian's head bowed and her shoulders drooped. "Then our agent has been compromised. Patch me through to the squadron so I can recall them."

"They left twenty-eight hours ago, Traveller. Angel's commanding officer left my ship behind as a precaution, but—"

"What class ship do you have, Angel? Even a small cruiser could keep the pirates bottled up in their base until the squadron returned."

"I'm just a patrol ship commander, Traveller. I'm sorry."

"Not your fault, Angel. Traveller out." Marian turned off the transmitter and hung her head. "It looks like you were right, Travis."

"I wish I wasn't," I said.

"Yeah, well, if wishes were warships..." Marian drew a ragged breath, released it, and then turned her usual controlled expression to me. "With Space Patrol out of the picture, you're in command, Travis. What should we do?"

A quick glance showed everyone else watching me. I straightened my posture and said, "We go with Trouble's suggestion, sneak inside the base, and scout around. But not all of us. Rita, you're our link to Ban, so you have to stay out here."

The mouth line on Rita's face screen turned down in a frown, but she said, "If you say so, Boss."

"Dave, you need to stay, too." Dave opened his mouth to protest, but I spoke first. "Someone has to teach the *amah'hashi* how to use blaster rifles."

Dave jerked a thumb at Marian. "Why not her? She's a better shot than me."

"Because she's the only person who can contact the Space Patrol agent inside the base. Besides, if this is Umna'Enle's tomb and Marian turns out to be Umna'Enle reborn, we might need her." Dave gave a reluctant nod, so I turned to Hu. "Hu, you must stay outside, too, and lead the *amah'hashi* once they arrive."

"I see wisdom in your words, Travis," Hu said, "but you are not my commander."

"Do as Travis orders," Inli'Ziyo said.

"Baxter, you'll also stay out here," I said. "Dr. Harmon and you are our only sources of knowledge about this tomb. We can't risk both of you at the same time."

Baxter didn't quite sigh with relief as he nodded. Harmon misinterpreted Baxter's emotion, clapped him on the shoulder, and said, "You have many years ahead of you, lad. I've no doubt you'll lead many dangerous expeditions in the future."

I addressed the team entering the tomb. "If Space Patrol's agent is compromised, we must assume the pirates are on the lookout for a search team like ours. Stealth is our only weapon."

"Until we find Insimbi'Vik," Inli'Ziyo said.

I had no reply to Inli'Ziyo's faith in the sword, so I had Trouble show him the location of the hidden entrance to the tomb. He and Hu planned our best route there, then Inli'Ziyo led us through a winding path, through gullies and behind boulders. Finally, Trouble led us through a narrow opening in the cliff face, about two hundred yards from the shielded base entrance. Then Trouble activated a dim light and led us deeper into the tomb.

My shoulders brushed smooth stone walls as I walked behind Trouble. The passage reminded me of the many narrow corridors found in the Space Patrol ships I served on during my five-year career. The racket of pirates preparing the *Bloodsword* for departure echoed down our passage, amplified by the close confines and the stone walls. After we had walked about a hundred feet, I caught Trouble's arm and stopped her.

I turned my back to the wall and waved Marian, Harmon, and Inli'Ziyo closer. Once everyone was close enough, I whispered, "We have two destinations, so—"

Marian's lips moved, but I heard nothing. Even though I'm no lip reader, I felt certain she'd said, "What?"

Next to her, Harmon cupped a hand behind one ear, showing he hadn't heard me either. Despite our distance from the pirates, their noise overrode my whisper. With a prayer that my normal tone wouldn't carry over the pirates's noise, I spoke normally. "We have two destinations. We can head for the main chamber, observe the pirates, and let Marian try to contact the Space Patrol agent inside. Or we can look for Umna'Enle's burial chamber and the sword."

Inli'Ziyo said, "Victory will elude us without Insimbi'Vik. We get the sword."

"The burial chamber must be our goal." Harmon agreed.

Neither response surprised me. I glanced at Trouble and lifted an eyebrow.

She considered the options for several seconds, then said, "I agree, but only if we scout the main chamber afterwards. We need to know what Inli'Ziyo's men will face when they attack the base. Won't we also have to figure out how to drop the force field?"

"Maybe," I said. "Or maybe we can bring the *amah'hashi* into the base through this passage and attack the pirates from behind." I turned to Marian. "Well?"

"Proper protocol says I should contact the agent, or at least try," Marian said. "Even if he's compromised, he's the only one who will receive the signal I would send."

"What if the agent has been turned?" I asked. "The pirates couldn't have sent the message luring Angel squadron away from Mars without his help. It doesn't matter if his help was coerced or voluntary. What matters is whether we can trust him to keep our presence secret after you contact him."

"My superiors in SPIF told me I could trust the agent with my life. But I also know everyone can be broken." Marian caught my gaze, and her eyes reflected far more of the vulnerable young woman than they did the trained SPIF agent. Marian glanced away and shook her head. "I... don't know."

"Magic swords aren't exactly part of my view of the solar system. But I would have said the same about Travellers and reincarnation before we left Marsport." I scrubbed my face with my right hand. "Even if there's no sword, we should learn what we can about this tomb's layout. Better we do that first, and then check out the main chamber." I looked at Trouble. "Do you... Does Inka'Tazo remember the way to Umna'Enle's burial chamber?"

Trouble considered my question, shrugged, and said, "Probably? Based on what's happened so far on this trip, I *think* I'll recognize the right way when I see it."

"Not the answer I was hoping for." I looked at Inli'Ziyo. "I don't suppose you remember the way?"

He spread his hands. "I remember much of Umna'Enle's life, but grief still clouds the details of her death. The route to her burial chamber is one of those details."

"Fair enough." I drew my blaster, made sure Trouble and Marian did the same, and then looked at Trouble. "Lead on."

We reached our first intersection three minutes later. Trouble considered the options before her and almost immediately selected the left corridor. She remained equally decisive the next four times the corridor branched. We'd been walking for almost fifteen minutes when she halted and turned around.

"I'm certain we're close to Umna'Enle's burial chamber." Trouble looked at me. "Any last orders?"

I raised my blaster, kept it pointed up, and thumbed off the safety. "Be careful."

Trouble nodded, disengaged her blaster's safety, and led us deeper into the dark corridor. Half-a-minute later, the corridor ended at a close-fitting stone door. Trouble shined her light along the left side of the door and then tapped something I couldn't see. With the soft grind of sliding stone, the door moved aside, and she led us inside.

After the close confines of the corridors, the dark chamber beyond felt vast. But my senses told me the room wasn't much over thirty feet deep and about as wide. Trouble's weak light revealed a sarcophagus near the far wall. Despite the distance and the poor illumination, I readily discerned the carved figure of a woman on the lid. And, clasped in her carved hands, the glint of a sword.

In quiet reverence, we walked towards the sarcophagus. When we reached the middle of the room, bright lights blazed to life all around the room, blinding us. I heard many feet rush towards us. Afraid of hitting a friend, I held my fire. Trouble and Marian must have felt the same as me, since neither of them fired, either.

Several men crashed into me, bore me to the floor, and disarmed me. From the sounds around me, I knew my companions suffered the same fate. Someone bound my hands and dragged me to the chamber's left wall. My vision cleared slowly, first letting me see my friends next to me. Someone turned off many of the lights, and I finally got my first look at our captors.

A mixed group of a dozen Martians and Earthers watched us. Unpleasant grins stretched their lips and morphed into disturbing leers when they looked at Trouble and Marian. Then a tall, muscular Martian walked into my field of vision. He carried a cloth sack, and his eyes sought Inli'Ziyo.

"I knew you would come for Insimbi'Vik someday, Inli'Ziyo." His eyes flicked to Marian. "But I didn't realize you would bring such a treasure as her with you."

The man opened the sack and withdrew something that glittered in the light. He gave a mocking bow to Marian and extended the glittering object. Light reflected from a thousand facets on a diamond carved in the shape of a heart. "I offered the Heart of Mars to you once before, when you were the goddess Umna'Enle. You spurned my offer then and gave your sword and your love to Inli'Ziyo."

"My God," Harmon said, "he must be Kan'Zima, from the tale I told during our first night on the canal boat, also reborn."

Kan'Zima's eyes shifted to Harmon. "How is it an Earther such as you know who I am?"

Harmon straightened his shoulders as best he could. "I am an archaeologist who specializes in Martian history. It's my *job* to know such things."

A genuine smile lit Kan'Zima's face. "You have read the ancient tales of our people?"

"Of course."

"Tell me, Earther, what do those tales say of me? Of my prowess in battle? Of my conquests?"

In a flat tone, Harmon said, "Nothing. Your name is mentioned once, as part of the story of Umna'Enle and Inli'Ziyo." Harmon's lips spread in a grim smile. "Beyond that, Mars has forgotten you entirely."

Kan'Zima's face went blank. He stepped in front of Harmon and drove the diamond heart into Harmon's face. Blood burst from Harmon's nose, his head snapped back, and cracked against the wall. Harmon's head lolled as Kan'Zima pulled his arm back for another blow.

"Stop it!" Marian cried.

Kan'Zima held his blow and looked at Marian. "You, who were once a goddess of Mars, would protect an Earther?" Marian responded with a white hot glare. A cruel smile split Kan'Zima's face. "When Mars most needs strength, you are still as soft-hearted as ever, Umna'Enle. How fortunate that I have strength enough for both of us. I lack only your sword."

"I will *never* give the sword to you!" Marian spat.

"Really?" Kan'Zima drew a knife and put it against Harmon's throat. "Not even to save this man's life?" He pointed at Trouble and me. "Or their lives?" He pointed at Inli'Ziyo. "Or the life of your eternally beloved?"

Marian looked away from Kan'Zima. "Please don't kill them."

"If I spare them, will you give me the blade?" Kan'Zima asked.

Marian nodded. "I will give you Insimbi'Vik."

fourteen
trouble with belief

"NO, you cannot give Insimbi'Vik to Kan'Zima!" Inli'Ziyo cried. "Do you not remember what he did after you chose me over him?"

"No, I don't." Marian's shields went up and her old, controlled expression returned. "I barely remember you. I don't remember Kan'Zima at all."

"Then I will tell you what I did after you gave Insimbi'Vik to Inli'Ziyo," Kan'Zima said. "I fought at his side against the invading horde."

"After your attempt to gain the sword, there is nothing else you could have done," Inli'Ziyo spat. "But after we routed them, you—"

Kan'Zima looked at his man nearest Inli'Ziyo and said, "I tire of his prattle. Gag him."

Inli'Ziyo leaned towards Marian and captured her guarded gaze. "I would unite our people. He would conquer—"

The gag cut off Inli'Ziyo's next words. But he held Marian's gaze, his eyes saying what his lips could not. Then Kan'Zima took Marian's bound hands, pulled her to her feet, and turned her head to face him.

In a low, intense tone, Kan'Zima said, "I would unite our people, too. With Insimbi'Vik in one hand and the helm of the

Bloodsword in the other, I will lead our people back to the glory that was once the birthright of all Martians." He pulled her into the middle of the room and turned her to face the sarcophagus and the sword. "Go. Draw the Insimbi'Vik. Say the words and give it to me." Kan'Zima untied Marian's hands. "And we will return our people, your *true* people, to the glory that once was."

Almost as if in a trance, Marian took slow steps towards the sarcophagus and the sword. Then she glanced at Trouble, and her steps faltered. Kan'Zima stepped between Marian and Trouble.

"Do this, and I will do more than lead our people to glory," Kan'Zima said. "Do this, and I will spare the lives of your friends."

Marian hesitated, nodded, straightened her shoulders, and strode purposefully to the sarcophagus. She took a deep breath and then grasped Insimbi'Vik's hilt with both hands. Her eyes widened in surprise or shock, or maybe both. Her body trembled. She released the hilt, stumbled away from the sword, and dropped to her knees. Marian huddled on the floor, her chest heaving, for what felt like an eternity.

Her body stilled. Her shoulders straightened. She lifted her head. And we beheld a face of radiant beauty. Marian's face, but different. Her face, but with something more. Something I couldn't describe to anyone who had not witnessed her transformation.

"I remember," she whispered.

"Are you okay, Marian?" I asked.

"Remember what, lass?" Harmon asked, his academic curiosity obviously more powerful than the threat of death hanging over us.

She looked at me. "I am fine, Travis. And I am no longer Marian. Or not *just* Marian." She turned her gaze on Inli'Ziyo. "I am Umna'Enle, daughter of two planets." Her eyes shifted to Kan'Zima. "Daughter of Em'Toen, the goddess of beauty." She rose to her feet with a grace Marian never possessed. "Daughter of Um'Vikeeli, the protector god."

"What else do you remember?" Harmon asked.

Her gaze never left Kan'Zima, and steel glinted in her eyes. "I remember everything, Dr. Harmon. Including Kan'Zima's crimes and treachery after Inli'Ziyo routed the attacking horde. I remember sending Inli'Ziyo to capture him. I remember Kan'Zima's trial. And I remember Kan'Zima's execution."

Kan'Zima maintained an impassive expression as Umna'Enle —I could no longer call the woman before us Marian—made her accusations. When she stopped speaking, he sneered. "If you truly remember me, then you know I do not make idle threats. Show us your true heritage, O Beautiful Protector." He waved a hand at the four of us still bound and propped against the wall. "Protect the lives of those you love by giving me Insimbi'Vik."

Umna'Enle and Kan'Zima matched glares. I guess Kan'Zima tired of waiting for Umna'Enle to break. Without looking away from her, he pointed to one of his men. "It appears I must make an example. Slit the throat of the older Earther man."

An Earther among the pirates grinned, drew a wicked knife, and twirled it in his fingers as he loomed over Harmon. Harmon met the pirate's glittering eyes with a glare that would have subdued any student in the solar system. As the pirate lifted his knife, Harmon straightened his shoulders, and even lifted his chin, baring his throat to the blade.

"Stop!" The haughty figure of Umna'Enle shrank into the all-too-human figure of Marian. "Stop. I'll... do it."

Kan'Zima held his hand, palm out, halting the pirate's descending knife. Disappointment flashed in the man's eyes as he sheathed his knife. Marian gave an indecisive nod, turned back to the sword, wrapped her hands around the hilt again, and pulled.

Nothing happened.

Marian set her feet and pulled again.

The sword didn't move.

"What are you waiting for?" Kan'Zima snapped.

"It... It's stuck," Marian said.

"Pull harder," Kan'Zima said.

Marian tried again. And again. Then she said, "I can't draw it."

"Why not?"

She shrugged. "I don't know. I mean, the sword has been here for hundreds of thousands of years." She looked at Kan'Zima. "You are a strong man. You could help me pull it out."

"You know what happens to anyone other than you who touches Insimbi'Vik. I have no death wish."

"I could give you the sword before we draw it."

Kan'Zima laughed. "Clever, Umna'Enle, but not clever enough. We both know you must physically give the sword to the bearer."

"Then you will have to live without Insimbi'Vik, Kan'Zima, for I cannot pull it from my sarcophagus's grasp."

Kan'Zima grunted in frustration, came to me, and yanked me to my feet. He drew his knife and slashed the rope binding my hands. He motioned to the same pirate who threatened Harmon, then pointed at Trouble. "Stand ready to kill the woman on my order."

Kan'Zima shoved me towards Marian. "Help her draw the sword, nothing more, or your woman dies. Do you understand?"

"Yes," I growled.

When I reached Marian, she said, "Put your hands over mine. That way, you won't accidentally touch the sword."

I stood behind her, wrapped my hands around hers, and braced my feet. "I'm ready when you are, Marian."

Without a word, she pulled on the sword. The blade slid easily through the sarcophagus's stone hands. As its tip came free, Marian whispered, "Shield my people with your wisdom and protect them with my blade."

Then she slipped her hands out from under mine. I, alone, held Insimbi'Vik.

The sword's grip felt as if it was made for my hand. The blade vibrated, as if from excitement, and almost felt alive. I waited for a flood of memories from previous lives, such as Marian received.

But none surfaced in my mind. Maybe I had no previous lives? Maybe it only worked for Martians? Who knew? Not me.

Reality crashed through my introspective split second communing with Insimbi'Vik when Kan'Zima cried, "Umna'Enle gave the sword to the Earther. Kill his woman. Kill her now!" Then Kan'Zima bolted for the door.

My gaze snapped to the pirate looming over Trouble as he drew his knife, raised it in one smooth motion, and grabbed her by the hair with his free hand. I could never reach him before he slashed Trouble's throat, but I charged him anyway.

"Yaaaaaahhhhhhh!" I yelled and slashed the air between us with the sword.

I had some vague hope simply swinging the magic sword would send the pirate reeling away from Trouble. It didn't. But the pirate turned his attention away from Trouble and to me. His eyes widened, he released Trouble's hair and flowed into a knife fighting pose. I don't know if the pirate realized his mistake, but his reaction gave Trouble the opening she needed.

Trouble rolled onto her back, spun her feet towards the pirate, pulled her knees up to her chest, and then kicked out with both feet. She aimed for the pirate's groin, but he'd turned his hips when he fell into the fighting stance. Her heels caught him on the thigh and sent the pirate reeling away from her.

The pirate regained his balance quickly, but I'd closed half the distance to Trouble by then. When the pirate saw Kan'Zima and the rest of his fellow pirates dash from the room, he threw his knife at me and then ran.

As if by its own volition, the sword twisted towards the spinning knife and knocked it aside. As the knife clattered on the stone floor, I started for the chamber's door. But the knife-thrower dove through the opening, and another pirate activated the door mechanism. Stone ground on stone as the door slid back across the opening.

I couldn't get at the pirates, but they couldn't get at me, either. I turned my attention back to my bound friends.

Umna'Enle—or maybe Marian, I couldn't tell anymore—retrieved the thrown knife. She freed Inli'Ziyo using the knife, while I cut Trouble's and Harmon's bonds with Insimbi'Vik. Then I took Trouble in my arms and held her.

"Are you okay?" I asked.

"I think I broke a nail," Trouble replied.

I laughed and squeezed her tighter. "Since when do you worry about broken nails?"

"All the time, back home on Carnegie Station. Not so much on a case."

"Then why bring it up now?"

"It was the quickest way to assure you I'm fine."

"You could have just said 'I'm fine.'"

"Yes, but then you'd have checked me over head to toe to make sure I wasn't making light of an actual injury. My way answered your question *and* told you I really am okay."

"I guess that makes sense..." I looked to Umna'Enle and Inli'Ziyo, who knelt with their heads together and murmuring, as Trouble headed towards the closed door. I coughed and said, "I'm sorry to interrupt a reunion a million years in the making, but we need to get moving before Kan'Zima overcomes his fear of the sword and comes back with a lot more men."

"I doubt Kan'Zima will return," Inli'Ziyo said. "He knows the power Insimbi'Vik's bearer wields and will want nothing more than to get away from us."

"Yeah, about that so-called power..." I said. "I didn't feel it when that pirate threatened Trouble."

"What did you desire above all else when you swung Insimbi'Vik?" Inli'Ziyo asked.

"I, um... I wanted to stop the pirate from killing Trouble."

"Which you did."

"But that was because I yelled at him."

"Was it simply that? Or did Insimbi'Vik make you appear more terrible than you imagine?"

I shrugged. "We can worry about that later." I turned to the woman at Inli'Ziyo's side. "Are you Marian or Umna'Enle?"

"I am both. Marian's memories burn brightest in my mind, but I have Umna'Enle's most cherished memories as well."

"Which name should we use?"

"Call me Umna'Enle. It is the name by which I'll be known after this."

"You're assuming there will be something after this. But there are fifteen hundred pirates against the five of us." Umna'Enle opened her mouth to say something, but I cut her off. "Yeah, I hold the sword. But I don't know what to do with it. Maybe I should give it back to you, so you can give it to Inli'Ziyo."

"No," she said. "You have a history with these pirates. So you must wield the sword against them."

"I agree with Umna'Enle," Inli'Ziyo said.

"I think you're making a mistake, but whatever." I headed for the door. "How do we open the door from this side?"

"We don't," Trouble said. "There's no opening mechanism on this side."

I glanced at Inli'Ziyo. "That seems short-sighted, in retrospect."

In a tone as dry as the Martian air, he said, "Are you suggesting I should have foreseen this situation thousands of lifetimes ago?"

"No, but—." I broke off as my comm buzzed. I pulled it out, accepted the call, and said, "Yeah?"

"Boss?" Rita asked. "We got problems out here."

"What problems?"

"A deep humming sound just started coming from inside the pirate base. Hayslett says it's the sound of a big spaceship beginning its startup procedure." Rita paused for a second, then added, "We don't know what you did in there, but Hayslett says the pirates must be prepping the *Bloodsword* for departure."

"Is there any chance Space Patrol can get ships to Mars in time to stop the *Bloodsword*?"

"Hayslett is on the tight beam to the patrol ship Angel squadron left behind right now. But it doesn't sound likely."

I bowed my head. To have come so close, only to fail at the last minute. A roaring filled my ears as the ghosts of my dead crew mates howled for justice, long denied. I howled with them and swung the sword at the door blocking our way. Insimbi'Vik struck the door and smashed it into a million pieces.

My gaze flicked back and forth between the remains of the door that once sealed Umna'Enle's tomb and the sword that shattered it. "How the hell?"

Inli'Ziyo clapped me on the shoulder. "Now, do you see the power of Insimbi'Vik?"

"Sure, but if the sword is that powerful, what difference does it make who holds it?" I asked. "I mean, couldn't you have smashed the door with it, too?"

"In time, yes," Inli'Ziyo said. "But not in time to pursue Kan'Zima and end his reign of terror."

"I don't understand." I turned towards the now-clear door-way. "But we can worry about that later. Right now—"

"Wait, Travis," Umna'Enle said. "You must understand Insimbi'Vik, or we have no hope of stopping the *Bloodsword*."

Inli'Ziyo nodded in agreement. Harmon's eyes gleamed with academic fervor at his front-row seat to potential historic events. I looked at Trouble. "What should I do?"

Her lips curved up in a gentle smile. "I think you already know the answer to your question."

I held her gaze for a moment, nodded, and raised the sword. "All right, Inli'Ziyo, how do I work this thing?"

"Insimbi'Vik draws power from its wielder's emotions. Deeply felt emotions produce vast power, power that dwarfs what you used to shatter the door." Inli'Ziyo's eyes lost focus, as if he stared into a great abyss. "Consider the canyon you Earthers call the Valles Marineris, my Martian brethren call *Umhos'ha Om'lu*, and which I named *Isilonda Sosizi*."

"Trouble said your name means Grief's Wound."

"And she is right." Inli'Ziyo's eyes regained focus. "Great was my grief. Greater was Insimbi'Vik's power. Far greater."

"Okay. I just need to feel something deeply and Insimbi'Vik does the rest," I said. "Got it."

"It's not that easy, Travis. Your emotions must connect to that which you wish to do." Inli'Ziyo paused for a moment, then asked, "What did you feel when you destroyed the door to this chamber?"

"I... hated coming so close to stopping the pirates, only to fall short because of a stupid door." I looked at the rubble scattered outside the doorway. "The ghosts of my crew cried for justice, and I swung the sword at the thing that blocked me from pursuing it."

"Do you understand now?" Inli'Ziyo asked.

"Yes, I think so." I gave a firm nod to him and then turned my attention back to finding a way to stop the pirates. I spoke into my comm. "You still there, Rita?"

"Yeah, Boss. I don't understand all the jabber between you and the Martian guy, but it sounds like you have a plan for stopping these pirates?"

"I hope so," I said. "But in case we need help, I don't suppose Ban has shown up with the blaster rifles?"

"He got here like fifteen minutes after you and Miss Boss went inside that tomb. He and Dave spent most of the time teaching Hu and some of his guys how to use the rifles."

"How many *amah'hashi* are there?"

"A couple of dozen. More show up every few minutes."

"Not as many as I hoped, but there's nothing we can do about that. Tell Hu to have his men ready to storm the base if the force field drops."

"You could come out here and tell them yourself, Boss."

"I can't do that, Rita."

"You can't stop a pirate gang with only five people, Boss. That's crazy!"

From nearby, Dave shouted something. His words weren't clear, but I assumed he was shouting at an *amah'hashi* who did something stupid with a blaster rifle. I ignored the shout, and said, "Got to go, Rita. I'm going to be busy, so don't try calling again."

Rita's voice rose two octaves. "But Boss—"

I canceled the call and tossed the comm to Trouble. "Hang on to that, okay?"

As Trouble pocketed the comm, I led our little band through the doorway. We picked our way through the debris from the door, and then we hurried down the corridor. I glanced over my shoulder at Trouble and asked, "Do you know the shortest way to the main chamber from here?"

"No, but I know *a* way to it."

"What about you, Inli'Ziyo?" I asked.

"That is not among my memories of my first life."

Out of habit, my eyes slid to Umna'Enle. A bit of the old Marian reappeared in Umna'Enle's expression, and she said, "Don't ask me. This is the first time I've been in this tomb. The first time alive, I mean."

"Trouble, just tell me where to turn," I said.

"Take the next left," she said. "Are you sure you don't want me to lead?"

We turned left and two pirates at the next corner opened up on us with blasters. I instinctively raised Insimbi'Vik and desperately wished I could protect Trouble and our friends. The sword flared in my hands and... ate the blaster bolts flying at us. I don't know how else to describe it. One second the air sizzled with white hot plasma, and the next the only thing left of the bolts was the flashing afterimage in my eyes.

One of the two pirates lowered his blaster and gave voice to my thoughts. "What the hell?"

The other kept shooting, even though Insimbi'Vik kept swallowing the bolts. Emboldened, I charged down the corridor. The vocal pirate turned and ran, but his buddy kept shooting at me even though none of the bolts hit. Just before I reached him, he flung his blaster at my face. Insimbi'Vik knocked the blaster aside, just as it did the blade thrown at me in the burial chamber.

I slashed at the pirate and the blade cut through his neck as if it were made of tissue paper. As the head rebounded off the wall, I turned to my companions. "Is everyone okay?"

"We're fine, Travis," Trouble called, as she and the others hurried after me.

"Fascinating," Harmon said, as he tried to run and write in his notebook at the same time.

I glared at Inli'Ziyo. "Why didn't you tell me the sword could absorb blaster shots?"

"I didn't know," he replied. "We didn't have blasters when last I held Insimbi'Vik."

"Oh. Um, sorry if I sounded accusatory." I started down the corridor again. "What else didn't you have back then, Inli'Ziyo?"

"Many things you take for granted, Travis," he said. "Space-ships, for one."

"Are you suggesting Insimbi'Vik can't do anything to stop a spaceship?"

"I'm saying I don't know. I believe it can, but it is not *my* belief that will be put to the test."

"So, no pressure, huh?" I muttered.

Trouble laid a hand on my arm. "I believe in you, Travis."

I caught her hand in mine and gave it a squeeze. "That helps."

And it did help. But would it be enough to end the *Bloodsword's* reign?

trouble with grief

WE RAN ON, following the only route Trouble knew to the tomb's main chamber and the *Bloodsword*. I heard the deepening thrum of a spaceship's engines starting two minutes after I slew the pirate in the corridor. The sound doubled my sense of urgency and lent strength to us all. Even Harmon, the oldest and least conditioned one among us, picked up his pace. It also gave Trouble certainty, and she no longer paused before selecting among branching corridors.

We ran for another ten minutes before she turned left into a long, wide corridor. The corridor ended fifty yards away, in a vast, brightly lit chamber. In the middle of the chamber, the *Bloodsword* sat in its docking cradle. A few dozen support personnel scurried around the ship, disconnecting hoses and releasing mooring lines. Most finished their task and ran into the closest airlock. Only a handful remained outside the ship when I burst into the massive chamber.

I called forth the ghosts of my friends and crew mates, victims of the *Bloodsword's* rampage through the solar system. Their cries for justice echoed through my mind. I raised my voice to join theirs. The few pirates still outside the ship turned my way, gaped for a second, and then ran for the nearest airlock.

But they waited too long. My cry turned into a howl as I

brought Insimbi'Vik crashing down on the floor. Cracks raced across the floor towards the pirate ship and the cavern shook. The men running for the airlocks staggered, and most of them fell. The lights illuminating the chamber went out, and the *Bloodsword* rocked in its cradle. At the far end of the chamber, the force field that blocked the chamber's entrance vanished. Martian sunlight stabbed into the tomb. And...

Dust swirled as the cavern floor steadied. The *Bloodsword's* startup sequence finished. Airlock hatches slid shut. Massive repulsors whined. I stared in horror as the *Bloodsword* slowly rose into the air.

Behind me, Trouble said, "The force field is down, Rita... Yeah, I figured you could see that... I don't know what use blaster rifles will be, but—"

A Space Patrol ship descended to block the *Bloodsword's* exit. The tiny ship—a mouse to the lion that was the *Bloodsword*—opened up with blaster cannons designed to clear space debris, not battle the most powerful warship in the solar system. My old ship, the *Soteria*, boasted stronger guns and better shields, yet the *Bloodsword* ripped her apart. Just one hit from a *Bloodsword* blaster cannon would blow the patrol ship to pieces.

Yet the patrol ship hovered before the mighty *Bloodsword* and spat tiny lances of white hot plasma over the *Bloodsword's* nose. The surprise attack, combined with my ground-shaking sword swing, caught the *Bloodsword* with her shields down. The little ship took full advantage of the situation and slagged the *Bloodsword's* forward sensor array. Two blaster cannon ports slid open on the *Bloodsword's* nose and the deadly guns extended.

Disbelief filled Trouble's voice as she asked, "What did you just say, Rita?"

The *Bloodsword* shrugged off further shots from the patrol ship. Without the forward sensors, the pirates had to aim manually. But their target floated a hundred yards in front of them. They simply couldn't miss.

The blasters belched searing bolts of plasma at the patrol ship.

And their target pulled off an all-but-impossible barrel roll up and over the shots.

Only one pilot in the solar system could have pulled off that move.

"He got the patrol ship commander to do *what*?" Trouble shrieked. She caught my shoulder. "Travis, Dave is—"

"Piloting the Space Patrol ship," I said.

As I spoke the words, Dave dodged another shot from the *Bloodsword*. But it wouldn't matter in the long run. No matter how well Dave piloted, the *Bloodsword* would destroy the patrol ship, and more brave souls would go into the great beyond.

"No," I whispered.

Dreaded memories surfaced.

"Euphoria, this is the SPS Soteria. What are your coordinates?"

"Thank God! Hurry! We think it's the Bloodsword!"

In the present, I whispered, "Not again."

"Comm? Send the Euphoria's coordinates and planned course to the rest of the squadron."

Lieutenant Power looked at me, a stunned expression on her face. "They're not coming."

"God, don't do this to me again!"

The weapons crew responded first. "We're with you, skipper!"

"Engineering is a go, sir!"

Alicia glanced around the bridge. "We're with you, too, sir!"

My vision blurred, and I blinked away tears.

My gaze swept across twenty-four coffins arrayed before me in the Space Patrol cemetery. Search and rescue recovered few bodies, so most coffins were empty. Visual symbols of the sacrifices made by my brave, loyal, doomed crew. Symbols provided for grieving family members standing mute behind me as the twenty-one gun salute echoed across the graveyard.

Tears overflowed my eyes and ran down my cheeks.

After the graveside service, Alicia Power's parents came to me. Her mother's lips trembled. Her father fought back tears as he asked, "Did our little girl suffer at the end, Captain Barrett?"

Unbidden, the memory of Alicia's hips and legs crushed flat under a massive console flashed through my mind, accompanied by her screams as the life drained out of her. I looked Mr. and Mrs. Power in the eyes and broke my most sacred personal vow. "No, sir, she didn't suffer."

"No more death!" I said.

The little patrol ship juked around another pair of blaster shots from the *Bloodsword* as the massive pirate ship began slowly gliding towards the exit.

"No more funerals!" I cried. My voice rose again as I yelled, "No more grieving families!"

The little patrol ship side-slipped and its blaster bolts raked the pirate ship. But *Bloodsword's* shields, now activated, flared as they stopped the shots. Despite the patrol ship's inability to even scorch the *Bloodsword's* armor plating, Dave didn't retreat.

"NO!" My voice crackled with emotion. "NOT AGAIN! NOT EVER!" I raised Insimbi'Vik over my head. *"IT. ENDS. HERE!"*

I swung with all my might. The sword hummed in my hands as it cleaved the air and struck the floor of the chamber for a second time. Stone exploded and giant fissures stretched like grasping fingers towards the *Bloodsword*. Tall, intricately carved support pillars collapsed as the fissures raced past them. Rocks fell from above the pirate ship, and the shields deflected them.

Then, with a mighty crack, the chamber's roof gave way. Thousands of tons of rock dropped on top of the *Bloodsword* and drove it to the ground. The *Bloodsword's* shields flickered as the falling rocks overloaded them. With an electronic snap and crackle, the pirate ship's shields failed.

Rocks kept falling for almost a minute. My friends and I stood safe, untouched by the devastation surrounding us. But the *Bloodsword* was gone. Buried under the weight of a mountain.

━━

TROUBLE WRAPPED her arms around me. "Are you okay?"

"Me?" I asked. "I'm fine."

"Sure, Travis," she said. "The emotions you channeled through that sword just brought a mountain crashing down on top of the *Bloodsword*. But you're fine."

I shrugged and maintained my stoic expression. "I'm better than Kan'Zima and the *Bloodsword*."

"Hey, this is *me* you're talking to." She took my head in her hands and forced me to look into her eyes. I saw love and concern for me reflected in them. "What are you feeling?"

I closed my eyes, drew a deep breath, and said, "I saw my crew die. Again. I buried them. Again. I lied about their suffering to parents and spouses and children. And I saw it happening all over again with that little Space Patrol ship." I opened my eyes. "I couldn't—wouldn't—let that happen again."

Trouble hugged me and held me tight. Then the comm in her hand came to life as Rita shrieked, "*Boss!* What happened? Boss? You can't be dead! You just can't—"

"We're fine, Rita," Trouble said.

"*Miss Boss!*" Rita cried. "How are you not—? I mean, the entire mountain just collapsed!"

"We're all fine, Rita. The sword protected us."

"There really is a magic sword, Miss Boss?"

"Sure is. I'll tell you all about it after we get out of here. Um, is the hidden entrance to the tomb clear, or did it get buried, too?"

"Hang on," Rita said. Her voice faded as she held the comm away from her vocorder and called to someone. Ten seconds later, she said, "Hu says it's clear. He also says you should get butts out of there before something else falls."

"We're on our way, Rita," Trouble said.

I caught Trouble's hand holding the comm and pulled it to my mouth. "And tell Dave I want to have a few choice words with him when I get out there."

Rita's tone brightened. "You got it, Boss! Can I watch you rip him a new one?"

"Yes, you can watch, Rita," I said. "We'll see you in fifteen or twenty minutes."

We turned to our companions. Trouble took the lead and started walking. I caught Umna'Enle's eye. "Sorry about wrecking your tomb."

Her lips spread in a radiant smile, so beautiful it almost hurt to look at it. "It's all right, Travis. As you may have noticed, I'm not using it at the moment."

Harmon cast a longing look back at the buried chamber and shook his head. "While I understand the necessity, losing the contents of that chamber breaks my heart. It must have held irreplaceable clues to ancient Martian history."

Trouble looked over her shoulder. "You realize you can just ask Umna'Enle or Inli'Ziyo about that history, don't you, Dr. Harmon?"

Harmon's eyebrows rose in obvious surprise. "By Jove—"

"Mars," Trouble corrected.

"Indeed, my dear," Harmon laughed. "By Mars, you're quite correct!"

"We'll be happy to answer your questions as best we can," Umna'Enle said. "But not until after we get some rest."

I suddenly remembered I still held Insimbi'Vik, and extended it hilt first to Umna'Enle. "Thank you for the loan of your sword."

She smiled but didn't take the hilt. "Why don't you keep it until we get outside? You've more than earned the right to bear my blade a while longer."

Fifteen minutes later, we reached the exit. Rita, Baxter, and the *amah'hashi* stood nearby. The Space Patrol ship sat on the ground behind them, with Dave and the dozen men and women who crewed the ship lined up next to it. Hu led his men in a cheer when we emerged, blinking into the Martian morning sunlight. They cheered even louder when they saw Insimbi'Vik, and louder still when Inli'Ziyo emerged.

Finally, Umna'Enle stepped into view, and what I can only call an awed silence fell over the *amah'hashi*. Almost as one, they dropped to one knee and bowed their heads. All but Hu, who grinned and said, "Welcome back, Umna'Enle. Your people have missed you."

A bit of the old Marian peeked out from behind the mortal goddess reborn, and her cheeks reddened. "Thank you, Hu. Thank you all. Please get up."

I caught Dave's eye and strode his way. Trouble hurried after me, and Rita bobbed along behind her.

The trepidation of a subordinate awaiting a dressing down by his senior officer filled Dave's face. "Look, Travis, I can explain!"

"Screw explanations!" I wrapped both arms around Dave and pulled him into a fierce hug. "Thanks, buddy. I couldn't have done it without you."

Dave gave me an awkward pat on the back. "Uh, done what, Travis?"

"Brought the mountain down," I said. "With this sword."

"You lost me."

"I'll explain it in a minute. First, how did you talk this ship's commander into coming down here and facing off against the *Bloodsword*? Not to mention letting you pilot?"

"I'm Lieutenant Commander Gail Elliot, captain of the *SPS Pathfinder*," a woman standing next to Dave said. "It was all my idea, Mr. Barrett. At least, I *think* it was my idea."

Dave smirked at me, turned to the ship's commander, and asked, "Please let me show him?"

Gail smiled and nodded. Dave reached over and removed her cap. Neck length red hair tumbled free. She gave her head a little shake and said, "I can't explain it, but..."

"Mars called you?" Trouble asked.

"Yes," Gail replied. "I know it doesn't make any sense, but—"

"I just collapsed a mountain with a sword," I said. "Mars calling you makes at least as much sense as that." I shook Gail's hand. "Thank you for listening to the call. And for stopping to pick up Dave."

Dave's expression turned somber. "I wasn't going to fail you again, Travis."

"You *never* failed me, Dave. So shut about that." Rather than let Dave dwell on his supposed shortcomings, I asked, "Are you ready to hear what happened in the tomb?"

I told and retold the story to everyone who asked to hear it— and everyone asked. Somewhere along the way, Gail returned to her ship and reported the destruction of the *Bloodsword* to both Space Patrol and Martian authorities. A joint delegation of

Martian and Earther diplomats—led by Mah'Ri—descended on our camp. And I retold the story several more times.

Martian authorities welcomed Umna'Enle and Inli'Ziyo with obvious joy and reverence. My fellow Earthers appeared unwilling to credit tales of souls reborn and magic swords, but at least they kept quiet about their doubts. It didn't hurt that Dr. Harmon corroborated everything we told them.

As the dinner hour approached, I made a big show of returning Insimbi'Vik to Umna'Enle. This time, she accepted it and immediately offered it to Inli'Ziyo. To everyone's surprise, he didn't immediately accept the sword.

"I will only take the sword if you consent to wed me again, Umna'Enle," Inli'Ziyo said.

"I will happily marry you," Umna'Enle said.

"Then do so tonight. Before my men and our guests." Inli'Ziyo took Umna'Enle's hands and stared into her eyes. "I have waited a thousand lifetimes for you. Do not make me wait another moment longer."

"I will," she answered, "but only if my troublesome friend, Inka'Tazo, will stand as my maid of honor."

Trouble blinked away sudden tears and smiled. "You already know my answer."

"Then it is settled," Inli'Ziyo said.

"Not quite." Umna'Enle looked at me. "Travis, will you act in my father's stead and present me to my husband to be?"

And so it was that Earth and Mars came together for a wedding a million years in the making.

sixteen
epilogue

DANCING, hard drinking, and increasingly ribald toasts followed Umna'Enle's and Inli'Ziyo's exchange of wedding vows. The shy maiden Marian part of Umna'Enle showed herself in the form of flaming red cheeks at the mildly risqué early toasts. But each sip of the potent Martian liquor loosened her inhibitions and, based on her bawdy replies, gave the decreasingly blushing bride access to memories of sexual experiences from thousands of Umna'Enle's past lives.

Finally, Hu rose from his seat next to Inli'Ziyo. The swaying second in command raised his hands, and the *amah'hashi* fell silent. The more reserved—not to mention more sober—Martian and Earther authorities stopped talking among themselves and also gave Hu their attention.

"History will mark this day as the greatest in the annals of the *amah'hashi*," Hu said. "Once again, Umna'Enle remembers her past. Once again, Insimbi'Vik defeated marauding foes. Once again, Inli'Ziyo bears the great sword. Once again, marital vows bind Inli'Ziyo and Umna'Enle. Once again, they will lead the people of Mars into a glorious, *united* future." Cheers erupted from the *amah'hashi*. Hu let the voices wash over the newlyweds for a moment, then raised his hands once again. Into the silence, he said, "But even such momentous events pale compared to the adventure that awaits Umna'Enle and Inli'Ziyo." Hu grinned at the couple. "Umna'Enle, lead our bold leader to his tent and have your way with him!"

Though her cheeks burned bright red once again, a laughing Umna'Enle rose, pulled her husband to his feet, and ran with him to their tent. As they ducked inside, Hu yelled, "I will post guards around the tent, and they will remain on duty until one of you dismisses them."

With the departure of the newlywed couple, the party quickly broke up into smaller groups. Some kept drinking. Others talked. A few of the least sober crawled off to sleep. And Mah'Ri sought me out.

"I held high expectations after I put my faith in you, Mr. Barrett." She smiled at Trouble and me. "But I never imagined you would exceed my expectations in such a spectacular fashion."

"I had a *lot* of help, Mah'Ri." I nodded to Ban, who sat laughing and drinking with Hu. "Not least from your own son. May I assume your government will clear his name and recognize his contributions?"

"They will," her voice filled with steely resolve, "even if I have to force them to do so."

"Is Ban the only person you'll do that for?" I asked.

"Of course not! I'll see these courageous *amah'hashi* feted across my world."

I turned my gaze to Dave, who sat nearby. He wore the infectious grin all the women loved, apparently including Lieutenant Commander Gail Elliot. She sat touching him, her head bent towards his, with laughter reflected in her eyes. "And?"

Intentionally or not, Mah'Ri misinterpreted my intention. "You may rest assured the young ship's captain will not suffer the indignities you suffered, Mr. Barrett. The governments of Mars will present her and her crew with awards for gallantry in defense of our world. Your Space Patrol will have no choice but to treat them as heroes after that."

"We appreciate that," Trouble said, "but Travis wasn't talking about the *Pathfinder's* captain and crew."

Mah'Ri watched Dave for a moment and then turned back to me. "I wonder if Mr. Hayslett understands how fortunate he is to have a friend such as you, Mr. Barrett?" She shook her head. "I can hardly believe he is the same man who almost drank himself into oblivion in my bar... But, to answer your question, I will see Mr. Hayslett's name honored by all Martians. Along with Dr. Harmon and his assistant, Mr. Baxter. And your names, as well."

"Don't forget the anonymous Space Patrol officer who infiltrated the pirate base. None of this would have happened without him." I glanced at our friends gathered around a campfire. "Make sure you add Rita to that list, too. She'll pout for days if you don't.

A Martian colleague called to Mah'Ri. She offered a last smile to us and joined the colleague. Two days later, the collective Martian governments conferred honorary Martian citizenship on us. Including Rita.

▭

A WEEK LATER, Trouble and I awoke in the apartment we shared. Instead of lazing about as we'd done every morning since our return to Carnegie Station, we bounded out of bed and took special care to make ourselves look respectable. That kind of thing came naturally to Trouble, and I benefited from her expertise.

When we met a casually dressed Dave at a nearby cafe, he gave a low whistle. "Whoa! Check out the station's newest power couple." As we sat down, Dave leaned towards Trouble. "You dressed him, right?"

"It's a big day," I said. "Of course she dressed me."

When we finished our light breakfast, Trouble asked, "You are going to stop by the office later and help us celebrate the grand opening of Travis and Trouble Investigations and Retrievals, aren't you, Dave?"

Dave shrugged. "I'll try."

"But?" Trouble prompted.

Dave looked down at the floor. "The, uh, *Pathfinder* docks in thirty minutes."

Trouble flashed her gigawatt smile. "And you haven't seen Captain Elliot in five days."

"Uh huh."

Trouble patted Dave's arm. "Tell her we said hi. And make sure you bring Gail if you find time to visit."

We waved at Dave and walked towards the office. Trouble's steps slowed as we neared the door, and she asked, "Do you think we'll have any clients?"

"There's only one way to find out," I said and pulled our office door open.

Three people stood before Rita's desk, all talking at once. Another eight people sat in the office. At the sound of the door opening, Rita turned her face screen towards us. It displayed a professional smile. As soon as she recognized us, the smile faded into a harried expression.

"Boss! Miss Boss! It's about time you got here," she said.

"We're right on time, Rita," I said.

"Yeah?" Rita waved to the potential clients, all of whom surged to their feet and began speaking when we entered. "Tell that to them."

Trouble waved for silence and got it. She offered a professional smile to everyone, and said, "Don't worry, we'll see each of you."

"I'll take the conference room," I said. "You take the office. That way, we can handle two clients at once."

As we headed for different doors, I said, "Rita, give us two minutes to get settled, then send the first two clients in."

"You got it, Boss," she replied.

I fixed two cups of coffee, handed one to Trouble through the door connecting the conference room and the office, and took a deep breath. Then the door from the outer office opened, and I met my first new client since Trouble walked through my door all those weeks ago.

about the author

Henry Vogel began his writing career in comic books way back in the 1980s, with the indie titles *Southern Knights* and *X-Thieves*. When the bottom dropped out of the black & white comic book market, Henry went into IT, where he worked for the next thirty-three years. Henry took up professional storytelling in 2006, and has performed all across his home state of North Carolina.

As a lifetime fan of science fiction, Henry always wanted to write science fiction novels. He began writing *Scout's Honor* in 2012, and released it to the world in 2014. He hasn't stopped writing since.

Henry makes his home in Raleigh, NC, and is hard at work on his next novel.

www.henryvogelwrites.com

also by henry vogel

Travis & Trouble

Trouble in Twi-Town

Trouble on Mars

The Fortune Chronicles

Fortune's Fool

The Scales of Sin & Sorrow

The Scout Series

Scout's Honor

Scout's Oath

Scout's Duty

Scout's Law

Scout's Training

Scout's First Mission

Hart for Adventure

The Princess Scout

Scout: The Lost Colony Adventures

Non-series books

The Lost Planet

Heart of Dorkness & Other Stories

The Connaught Family Chronicles

The Fugitive Heir

The Fugitive Pair

The Fugitive Snare

www.ingramcontent.com/pod-product-compliance
Lightning Source LLC
Chambersburg PA
CBHW061736310726

48969CB00002BA/705